I0638928

revolution radio

by Seth Kenlon

01.01.00

Abstract

After The Revolution.

Anarchy reins supreme, there are no laws -- and it's working. People are building cities and living off the land and doing whatever their passion prompts them to do. The land and its resources are governed by a set of ancient documents known only as the "GPL", the "CC", and "Berkley's Law".

The Comm Techs.

They're called "commies" for short; they run all the communication in the world, exclusively by radio and a device known as the Konsole. The commies don't socialize much; they just broadcast information, and monitor it, and archive it. It's a regional system, and they're keeping it that way because global communication is considered a thing of the "old world".

The New World.

One commie has a secret: she used to be a member of a controversial revolutionary group dedicated to making sure nothing from the Old World survived after the Revolution was won. But now she's just a commie, up on her mountain Perch, alone. She spends her days listening to broadcasts, archiving information, and maintaining her radio tower.

And then one day, the daily broadcast doesn't come. Radio silence.

And it's up to her to go find out why.

revolution radio

seth kenlon

ISBN 978-0-984-7842-1-9

Chapter 1. Comm Shack

> The revolutionary is a doomed person with
> no personal interests, no business affairs, no
> emotions, no attachments, no property, and
> no name. Everything in the revolutionary is
> wholly absorbed in the single thought and the
> single passion for revolution.
>> — The Revolutionary's Catechism

My encampment was simple.

Most days, I could see for miles and miles into the distance until
the spinning arms of the windmills blocked the horizon from
view. But then I would just turn around, and look in the other
direction, past my auto-hut, and look in that direction.

All I needed in life was an auto-hut, food, and water. And maybe
a rifle, just in case. But that's all anyone really needs.

Sometimes I want something else. I want someone to come
walking up the road, a smile on their face. I want to invite them
to sit down, have some tea and something to eat, and talk.

At one point, there'd been neighbours and neighbourhoods.
There still were, I guess, but not around me. I'd gotten away
from those things a long time ago.

That morning, I returned One. A simple little message letting
the station over the horizon that I hadn't gotten a signal.

```
wall
```

```
missing sig -o
```

Simple as that. There was no immediate answer, so I left the
little konsole and had breakfast.

I liked to eat on the Perch so I could watch the landscape around
me. I ate simple things, mostly oats and dried fruit, and whatever

greens I could grow in my garden. Very rarely did I indulge in any special food, and not just because I had a limited supply of that; I didn't indulge because I didn't care to indulge.

Self-indulgence is something we just don't do much any more, we humans. I guess some of us have adopted something called self-denial. When you want something, see how long you can go without it. Or see if you can come up with a creative way around to getting whatever it is about it that appeals to you. Or go and get it, and then give it away to someone else, for free, without anything in return.

These were drastic, new ways of living. Not everyone wanted to live this way, but most of those people had died off or had eventually come around to that way of life.

So when a human wants something, it's a badge of honour to not have it. It shows resolve and restraint. It shows a higher consciousness.

Someone noticed, a long time ago now, that if a human wants something, it's usually because they want whatever that thing provides them. Humans don't usually really want something just for the materials that it consists of. They want what it provides.

Watching people down on the plain, on the rare occasion that there are people on the plain, if I wanted to send them to the great Devnull, I wouldn't have really wanted a bullet; I would have wanted somebody's head to explode. Granted, a bullet would provide me with that result, but if I didn't have a bullet, that wouldn't have been an option. Therefore, as a human, I should be able to find another way to make someone's head explode, or their heart to be forced out of their chest, or their throat to be ripped apart, or whatever will result in a quick and timely death.

And that's the mark of a human with resource.

But I'm not a crank, so I wouldn't have wanted these things anyway.

But if I say I want a new rain-cover for my auto-hut but my rain-cover works just fine as it is, then I am seeking a result that I already possess. That is to say, I don't really want a rain-cover, I really am seeking to keep rain out of my hut -- but the rain is already kept from my hut, so why am I desiring a new rain-cover? The answer is that I am seeking the satisfaction of going out and constructing or finding a new rain-cover. If I go do this, then I'll have two rain-covers in the end, which I do not need, and so the thing to do is to find someone with an insufficient rain-cover and give it to them. End of story.

That is the mark of a human with rectification.

And generally speaking, those are the three traits that make us Human.

Restraint, resourcefulness, and rectification.

I sent another message on the konsole.

diff computers humans

I didn't hit ENTER, because I didn't want to see it actually Return One. I just hit control-c and imagined

Return Zero.

Chapter 2. Perch

The plains were empty, the air silent, and the sun strong. That's how it had been for a very long time.

I was sitting on my Perch. I call it my Perch because that's what I do there, I perch. It used to be what they called a Scenic Overlook. A place for motorists to stop on their way to a campground, maybe, and look out at the world beneath them. Like they could see everything from there.

I used it as a watchout. I watch that empty plain every day, and it's always empty. Once, a few moon cycles ago, a truck drove across the plain, trailing dust behind it as it sped across my world. The truck had been going fast; too fast, because about midway across it hit an unexpected ridge and blew a tire. It tried to keep going, but pretty soon they had to stop.

When they did, you could tell they didn't like it. A lot of people got out and they all had guns. And they all looked around nervously, covering the mechanic that got out to change the tire.

I know these things, because I was watching them like I was right next to them, peering through my Broehm-88 sniper scope. I guess I could have killed all of them from where I was. The Broehm-88 has an unnatural range, I could have shot them at my leisure and they could never have reached me, at least not with the guns they were carrying.

But I'm not a killer any more. I'm just a commie. I listen to radio signals, I keep my tower in working order, I make sure the broadcasts are received and get sent back out on schedule. I fix stuff when it gets broken. That's pretty much what I do.

When you see people from up on a mountain, they're small and don't look like real people. But if you look at them through a scope, you see their faces, you see their muscles move beneath their skin, you see them do human things, like blink, or swallow, or scratch their head, or bite their lip.

Sometimes

they even smile.

When the truck's tire was fixed, which took no time but probably felt like a little eternity to the people with the guns, they all piled back into the truck and it kept going. A little slower, but not by much.

I'd expected, then, to see another truck or a series of trucks pursuing the first. I think they probably were expecting that. But I waited there on my perch, watching, and nobody came. It was just the same old empty plain as usual.

Quiet,

and vast,

and eternal.

Even when it was disturbed, it only took a few moments to erase that from its history, and continue on in solitude and peace.

Chapter 3. Rain

> The revolutionary knows that in the very depths of the being, not only in words but also in deeds, all bonds have been broken which would tie the revolutionary to the social order and the civilized world with all its laws, moralities, and customs, and with all its generally accepted conventions. Their implacable enemy, if a revolutionary continues to live with them it is only in order to destroy them more speedily.
>
> — The Revolutionary's Catechism

When it rains, I stay in my auto-hut and watch the landscape.

Rainy days are good for cleaning. I hang out all my clothes, so the rain can soak them through. I set out my plate, mug, and utinsil set. And in my hut, I cleaned out my Broehm sniper, my Springfield close-range rifle, and my Smith and Wesson handgun. And I generally straightened out my hut, a converted van, or something like that.

I guess my hut had probably seen a lot of action in its time. I'd painted it dust brown with some old paint I'd found in a surplus post, but when I found it, it had been red once, and it had had an emblem on it that no one knew any more. It had over 300,000 miles on its counter, so I knew it had been well used, probably mostly after the Revolution.

After the Revolution people started discovering their inner resourcefulness. Whereas people needed a new automobile every five years before, suddenly people found they could make do with any old automobile for pretty much their entire life. And eventually, once nearly all of the automobiles had truly become useless, they all got repurposed in the auto-villages. I've never seen an auto-hut become obsolete, unless it was abandoned. But as long as someone is in it, they seem to pretty much be good forever. Where "forever" is a relative term.

I'd found my automobile out on the side of the mountain, near an abandoned campsite. I stayed in the area for the rest of that moon cycle, and then a complete one after that, and nobody came back to claim it. But I didn't like the location, and I didn't much care for the idea of someone coming back to it and insisting it was still theirs and getting angry about it. Angry people do irrational things, so I decided to put some distance between myself and that former location.

I had to push the van up the mountain a lot more than I care to admit, and for a lot longer, too. But I was in no hurry. I went up to the top every morning to tend the konsole, and then I'd come down to push my van. Back up to tend the konsole, back down to push my van. I did this until I was so sick of it that one day I finally just pushed until I was exhausted. Then I collapsed in my new auto-hut and slept all the way through the evening and night until well into the next morning.

Building an auto-hut isn't hard. There were instructions on the konsole if you didn't know how. I'd seen people do it before. I made a canopy, and a porch, and I arranged the seats to my liking. It was still red on the outside though, and eventually I painted it to match the surroundings. I found some sheet metal to put over the windows at night.

I still need to shape that sheet metal. Some chores you just never get around to.

For a good long while, after all the cleaning, I sat on my covered porch, playing a guitar I'd found a long time ago, watching the rain come down. Little droplets, falling from the sky, crashing into the dirt. It made the whole ground ripple sporadically. It didn't seem like nature's usual method of doing things. It didn't come in waves or in undulations, it came at random, disturbing things on the ground with inconsistent timing.

The rain stopped, but there were still no transmissions on the konsole. I figured since it had rained there should have been at least a weather report. But it was completely dead.

I went out to the Perch and closed the water collectors. And then I sat in my wet chair there and watched the land below me. It was full of rich wet colours now, and as the clouds parted and sun broke through these colours changed and sparkled, but the land itself was empty as ever. Devoid of life or movement. As it had been ever since that auto had blown a tire and continued on its way.

I felt lonelier than I had in a long time.

It didn't help, I think, that I wasn't receiving any comm signals.

It hadn't happened before, but when such a thing happens, it was really expected of me that I figure out why.

Pondering it a little, I ascertained that it could only be a few things. There were steps to find these things out, tests to run. So I ran them. I looked at the konsole. I looked at the antenna. I looked at the physical connection between the two. But everything there on my mountaintop was working. There were no malfunctions or suspicious responses to tests. If there were signals flying through the air, the equipment built there on the top of the mountain would be picking them up.

But there was nothing, so I left the konsole in Listen and went back to my auto-hut.

Chapter 4. The Godstream

What can be heard from an open portal like a konsole set to Listen surprises everyone the first time they hear it. There is the usual static, signals being bounced down onto the planet from outer space, and then reverberating over the entire landscape and back off the atmosphere, and back again. A radio, somewhere, singing simple songs made by someone with a guitar and whatever voice they could summon up to sing into whatever radio box they had come across. Old news broadcasts, looping from some unknown and forgotten tower on automatic. And the Godstream. The pulsing, ever-flowing and ebbing Godstream.

I'd listened to that more than my fair share. I could tune into it whenever I wanted to, both literally and figuratively, and there I was.

One with the Godstream.

I had hours and hours of Godstream recorded. Every so often I had to use up one of the tape drums for a system backup of "real" information. But there were a few tapes that I'd shelved, with just Godstream on them.

I heard Godstream in the rain. When it had started raining, last night, I sat in my auto-hut as usual, listening to the rhythm-less tap-tapping of the raindrops, and honestly, there were times when I could pick it out. But they were fleeting moments, just brief glimpses of it.

The rest of the time I just laid on the sofa, staring up at the blank ceiling of my auto-hut, but not sleeping. Not even thinking; just laying, and listening.

Most people do that now; they listen a lot.

Used to be nobody listened. You'd hear it in arguments. I've heard old radio shows. Romance shows, about relationships, and the girls would call in and say "My boyfriend never listens to me" and then her boyfriend, conveniently right there on the other line, would get on and say "I listen to you, baby" because that's how they used to talk, "I listen to everything you say." So the girl would say something like "Then how come when we were out last Friday night and I was telling you about how my boss was treating me and I asked you what I should do, you had no idea what I had even said?" and her boyfriend would say, "Huh?" and then bells and whistles would play and the show's hosts would rant and rave and by the end of it, the girl and her boyfriend weren't even on the line any more. They'd just evaporated. They were gone, like they'd never existed.

But people listened for that girl and boy now. They listened for the dead space, the unsilent void, the Dev Null, where these glimpses of people got sent to. They were probably still there right now. Still talking and not listening. Alive, but in limbo.

But we listened for them. We all did.

"Come back to us," we were saying, every time we fired up a radio station. Come on back and yammer again. Tell us about your problems. About your petty, simple-minded disagreements. Hint at the happy times, but tell us about the trouble you're having.

I'll tell you what problems are. They're having a Springfield shoved into your nose in the middle of the night, not knowing if the Crank on the other end is going to pull the trigger or just send you packing. That's a problem. Problems are finding out there's a subgroup on the plot of land you've just wandered onto. Yes, now these are problems. Problems are building up the gnu world order with a solar panel, a bike-powered battery, and an 8 season's supply of dried apples, nuts, and random jarred vegetables.

"Problems worth solving," I said, accidentally aloud. Sometimes I do that. Sometimes after a year of having nobody to talk to, you just say things aloud so as you can agree with yourself.

"I don't want to have to shoot nobody," I said to the ceiling. "Not now, not never."

I sighed and relaxed, and I heard the Godstream in the pattern of the rainfall. And that was how I knew, deep down, that I was going to have to leave my mountaintop and find out why I wasn't receiving those daily transmissions any more.

Chapter 5. Children of Elektronix

> The Society has no aim other than the complete liberation and happiness of the masses – i.e., of the people who live by their own labor. Convinced that their emancipation and the achievement of this happiness can only come about as a result of an all-destroying popular revolt, the Society will use all its resources and energy toward increasing and intensifying the evils and miseries of the people until at last their patience is exhausted and they are driven to a general uprising.
> — The Revolutionary's Catechism

The Children Of Elektronix is what the subgroup had called itself. We got broadcasted, and after that it never was really the same again. And I guess that above all else is what brought it all to a crumbling halt. That was what caused the cave in. The breakdown of all our relationships and a cessation of harmony. A simple broadcast. Just like what we had all been fighting against in the first place.

It both proved our point, and destroyed us all at the same time.

I can't speak for the others, but one thing I can say for certain is that it had destroyed me. It tore me apart, and left me to deal with myself. That was something that, let's say, I'd been ignoring for a while.

Choosing to become a commie and actually man a comm tower was maybe a little unexpected, but for me it was just something I knew I could do, and it gave me the opportunity to spend time alone, which I knew I needed. I needed it then and I think I'd needed it up until very recently.

Pangs of loneliness were new for me. It wasn't something I was used to, not for a long time. I had been perfectly happy on my mountaintop, tending my garden, tending my repeater tower, listening in on random transmissions, sitting out on my perch, watching the emptiness.

The call of the People was loud, though, in its absence. There was no good reason not to be receiving comm transmissions, not even a response to my inquiries. Something was wrong, and it was part of the job I'd taken to find out what was wrong. I put it off for as long as I conscientiously could manage, and then the curiousity and loneliness got the better of me.

A cantine full of water, my Springfield rifle strapped to my back and my Smith and Wesson on my belt, and some clothes and supplies in a backpack, and I was on the road again after what seemed like an entire life alone on my mountaintop.

I set off toward the sunrise, down my lonely mountain, and toward the Dev Null of the signal that once was. There had been no news of any great catastrophic event, or any signficant change, but for all I knew, I was the last person on Earth. It was like, and I do say "like", everybody had gone and vanished into thin air, like the boy and girl arguing on the radio after the radio host took over the show again.

Then again, if they'd vanished into thin air it might have been better because then at least I'd have heard them on the airwaves. But as it was, there was nothing. Just emptiness.

It was into that emptiness that I travelled for the first time, in a long time. The land hadn't changed much from what I remembered. Of course, for the initial few miles I assumed correctly that I was walking on land that I'd been able to monitor from my mountaintop. But it had all stayed pretty well the same as I remembered from when I'd walked up the mountain so long ago. No settlements had cropped up. When I'd found the mountain, and after I'd repaired the relay tower, I had taken quite some time to ensure the road up the mountain was blocked without looking like it had been intentionally blocked. It hadn't been easy work, but some dynamite and an axe made it possible.

I'd known all about explosives by then. By that time, I'd blown up quite a wide variety of things. I knew how to handle them, where to place them for maximum efficiency, and how far away to be so that I didn't either blow up myself or crush myself with debris.

Contrary to what some might think, learning about specialized equipment that is rudimentary like explosives and guns is not difficult. It boils down to practise. Blow enough objects apart, and you'll know everything there is to know about how explosives work. And in fact, you'll have more pragmatic knowledge than someone who might know how to make them. You might not know how to make them (or, then again, you might) but you will certainly know where to place an explosive to blow off a chunk of mountain, or where to place it if you want to blow up a vehicle cleanly rather than blowing it up and creating dangerous shards of shrapnel.

It's the higher level things, the more abstract tools, the creative and productive ones, that are more difficult to master. For instance, if building a solar power array from materials found in an old junkyard was easy, I don't see why people wouldn't be building them all day long.

The Children of Elektronix built things. We'd built all kinds of electronic wonders, with the parts of old machines we found lying around in the old cities. But we also destroyed things. We'd destroyed things in many different ways. We destroyed people, we destroyed spirit, we destroyed machine, and we destroyed history.

I felt those were important things to destroy. I guess I haven't changed my mind about that. I still think we destroyed things that needed to be destroyed.

But somehow we'd all ended up destroying ourselves, and each other. Some might say that was the price of revolution. I say it's the price of fame. If you ever stage a revolution, do it quietly and completely.

Every time I see a structure from the old world still standing, in tact and overly-grandeous, I cringe and take mental note. I think "Next revolution, be sure to blow that building to pieces first thing."

At some point, buildings stop being mere functional structures for shelter or containment. They become symbols, statements of an architect's desire to be unique and outstanding, or a statement of a politician (that is what they used to call a Crank in power), or a monument to the Rich, and so on.

The very layout of some of the old cities was in itself a statement. If a man is judged to be evil, and we assume every cell in his body is evil, then the inverse of that is true for cities. The individual buildings are reprehensible, and the way the buildings stand in relation to one another is a statement of apathy and greed. Think about this: cities were most often not designed at all, and the design that emerged was a haphazard self-serving design for the men using the city for their own profit. The fact that there was a downtown and a City Hall (centers of local government) and expensive "premium" housing quarters nearby, and the obligatory cottage industries of expensive restaurants and entertainment places where women would be forced by way of poverty to dance naked for these lecherous men, and useless, gratuitous things like movies and music were played only for a price; these all betray the focus of every city. The whole body that was the city was a self-sustaining monument to avarice, with the poverty-stricken people existing only to maintain it for their rich masters-who-were-not-masters. And of course this impoverished majority was stupid enough such that they too became dependent upon the monument, such that if the city were to fall then they would all die along with its Rich owners. So they continued to maintain their own disease.

Cities used to have literal undergrounds, and outskirts, to which the poor would be relegated. I often found that a humourous historical joke, that the poor who maintained the churning cities were never actually able to dwell in the city proper. There was a real physical separation whenever possible. Tall, "sky scraping" buildings housed the rich. They were in their "penthouses", on the rooftops, far above any of the menial janitors of their city. Just like me, and my mountaintop, my Perch. So far above and away from everything that it had ceased to exist. Sometimes, you really believe that; you really think that because something is so far gone from your awareness, your thoughts, and your presence, that it simply must not exist any longer.

But now everything was starting to exist again, because I was walking down the side of my mountain, back into the fray. I found myself wondering what really did exist now. Maybe nothing did, maybe I was right. Maybe they'd all puttered out, evaporated into the radio silence. And if that were the case, it was all one with the Godstream now, and that was one thing I'd always have as long as I had a receiver. And me. I'd always have myself.

Chapter 6. Transmissions

I walked in the direction of the sunrise until the sun was setting behind me. I started looking for a spot to camp, and found one easily enough. There was a little clearing by the road, with some trees around it to block the wind when there was wind, and what was clearly a pit for a fire. It was probably a common campsite, something vaguely maintained by each person who happened across it. These places were known as GPL land, which was an acronym that stood for something but no-one really knew what. What it really meant was that the land was to be shared among everyone, belonging to no-one and to everyone simultaneously. The idea was simple, and in fact it applied to a lot more than just campgrounds; leave the site better than you found it, and always share it with anyone who happens by.

I hadn't seen any other travellers all day so I didn't expect any visitors. I made a campfire from some dead branches among the trees around me. I didn't need a fire for warmth, but I felt like a little light.

I ate some fruit and crackers, drank some water, and then sat down ostensibly to drift off to sleep. I'd walked all day and was tired from it.

Yet I could not sleep. Maybe I was missing that old familiar version of Auld Lang Syne, that I hadn't heard in days, to lull me to sleep.

Sitting there, on the ground that I used to only look at from high above my mountaintop, I felt strange. Like I'd come back to a time and place I hadn't really ever intended to come back to. And it was jolting me with random memories that I could not control. Sitting there in the darkness, I could almost hear the daily transmissions.

```
KCG 1,2 cloudy with a chance of
rain, KTN 2.7 sunny with chance
of night showers. KPA 3,3 sunny
and a balmy 28 degrees
```

And on and on, until the weather was finished. And then they'd start the activity notices.

```
KCG  1,3  surplus  of  power
distributed  back  to  1,2 grid
KCG 1,2 surplus of power traded
to  0,8  for  water  KMA  4,8
possible cranks violation of GPL
farmland,  possibly  same  group
of  cranks  as  reported  last
week  in  6,8  KPA  3,3  initial
reports of improved battery life
in  central  solar  tower,  tests
ongoing,  reporting  as  per  CC
license
```

And on it would go through all of any interesting news towns had to report. Failing to report interesting news was usually considered some kind of violation and, while there was nothing anyone could do about that, there was the general sense that violating the "law of the land" would result in less cooperation from other towns when your own town was in need of something. It seemed fair.

And then the data stream would come on; a series of garbled eratic blips and pops and tones that most people could not distinguish from Godstream. But commies knew the sounds, and their konsoles picked up the information. This would contain all the information just broadcast, compressed and archiveable, plus the less interesting updates on each town, such as expense reports and births and deaths and things like that.

We didn't like to talk about birth or death. Used to be a big celebration, before the Revolution, whenever someone was pregnant, born, or got absorbed by the great Dev Null. Now we treat it more like a comm signal. A transmission appears. A trasmission fades. It's only natural. We don't feel the need to mask our confusion about it with feigned excitement and glee.

The daily transmissions would, finally, play the appropriate ending song. "Waltzing Matilda" for the morning broadcast, and "Aulde Lange Sine" for the evening broadcast. It was always the same version, providing a consistent end for each broadcast. Absurdly, it gave everyone who heard it structure and comfort.

Sometimes there would be this sort of transmission:

```
KVT  2,2  requests  change  in
morning  broadcast  end  song,
suggests Pennsylvania Polka as
suitable replacement.
```

And that's the last you'd hear of that. At this point, it was more or less a joke among commies. Something to insert into your stream if you had nothing better to say or just got bored. Because as everyone knows, all requests to change the logout songs were sent directly to /dev/null.

Sometimes you'd hear other requests, too. Things like particular people in need of some sort of supply that the town, for whatever reason, simply did not have access to. If it was a life-or-death situation, the transmission got bumped to the top of the list without question, and it got broadcast pretty much all day and all night, except during regular broadcast hours, until it was filled. No one liked this, because re-broadcasting meant you needed power. All day and all night. So the sooner the supply was obtained, the better for everyone.

Before the revolution, things were broadcast all day and all night as a matter of course. They were generally selling things. And if someone needed help, they would have to pay to be on the radio. And they'd have to pay premium prices. But sometimes someone would pay for them, and in paying for the message, they got to put an extra transmission in the stream, and they could sell more of whatever it was they were trying to sell. "No one ever said you wouldn't have to give a little to get a little", they would say. Now we say you have to give until someone else gets, end of story. Life, first. Everything else existed only to support that. And until someone found a good way to deal with the birth and death issue, with the delay it took for supplies to reach the living people in need of them, and things like that, there wasn't going to be any development of luxury items or exciting forms of entertainment, or anything like that. That's what we call Communal Focus.

Funny thing is, no-one really knows how anyone gets the jobs they have in a town. Some people grow into them, others seem to be born into them, others stumble across them. And if you want to see a time where we can listen to Pennsylvania Polka at the end of the broadcast instead of Waltzing Mathilde, you'd better figure out how to get emergency supplies across vast stretches of land instantly. When you do that, we'll change the tunes. That's what the commies said. And I guess we meant it, because we haven't backed down yet.

Chapter 7. Farmland

The next day when I woke, I cleaned up the campsite, made sure the fire was out in the pit, left a can of beans as a tip, and continued on my way. I felt like, that day, I would find some civilization.

It wasn't just a feeling. I knew civilization couldn't be much more than a day's walk in any direction. I knew this because I was a commie and I knew the grid.

So I kept walking in the direction of the sunrise, and about midway through the morning a truck drove past me. I waved at it but it didn't stop, it just kept driving. I didn't get a good look at anyone inside, mainly because its windows were too dusty to see in, and the sun was still in my eyes. It hadn't been moving terribly fast, so I assumed it was maybe a transport to another town in the area. But whatever it was, it meant I had to be close to some group of people somewhere.

I walked well into the afternoon, and finally came upon what was clearly an in-production farm. There were fresh bales of hay in the field, and the land felt alive. I kept walking until I happened upon the proper entrance, and turned there to go see who was tending the land and to get whatever information I could.

Commies were kind of known for their ability to get information. I'd had a day and a half to formulate some stories and questions.

When I was far enough in, I started encountering people. Everyone was working their shift, no-one of higher rank or importance than anyone else. It was GPL property, and doing fine.

A big man came toward me and spoke: "You lookin' for work, mister?"

At first I didn't know who he was talking to, until I realized that he thought I was a young male.

I cleared my throat, contemplating whether I should try to deepen my voice and pass myself off for a male or not. I didn't try. At the same time, I hadn't really heard my voice in such a long time. Sure I'd said a few things here and there, but not to another person. Not for a very long time.

"Not work, not now. Just lookin' for a commie."

"We don't got a commie here. You want to go into town for that. KCG, over that-away."

"Yeah I know KCG, I'm from there," I said.

"Why'd you come here then, for a commie?" he asked.

"Traveling from another grid. I didn't intend to go back to KCG but if I have to, to find a commie, I guess I will."

"It's not much farther," he said. "You'll reach it tomorrow morning, or if you travel at night you can reach it overnight."

"I'd rather not," I admitted. "You got an extra bed? I'd be glad to help out here for the rest of the day, and go on my way tomorrow."

"Yeah we probably got space," he said. "I don't see why not, anyway. Come on, I'll show you where you can stash your stuff and find something for you to do."

He wiped his face of sweat with a rag, which he then tossed back over his shoulder, and lead me into the big farmhouse not far ahead.

Inside, it was homey and comforting. Compared to my auto-hut, it was a palace. Everything was well-kept and clean. There were people in the house, some having finished their shifts earlier in the day, others doing house chores for their daily work. I looked around for some matron of the house, some big kind woman that would make me think of my own mother. I expected it, in that environment. But there was none. And that made me happy.

My guide showed me to a room with bunks in it. A top bunk had some things on it, which he gathered and put on his own back. "There you go, that's mine. You can have it tonight, there's a couch out in the living room I'm fond of."

"I couldn't possibly take your bed," I said. "I can sleep on the couch."

"You're a guest, you sleep in the rack. I won't miss it for one night."

"Thanks," I said. I put my backpack and guns on the bunk.

"What kind of work do you do?" he asked. "We got lawn care we're doing now, or house chores here, cooking. The usual. I don't know if you ever worked on a farm before?"

I shook my head. "No I'm just a handyman. I can fix stuff, if you got anything that's broke. Otherwise, I can do yard work."

"I don't think any thing's broken right now," he said. "We have a pretty good handyman here, she can fix about anything you give her."

I reached into my backpack and took out an old circuit board. "How about this? Can she fix one of these?"

He looked at it, shrugged. "I don't know what that is. Doesn't look broke to me. But we can ask her. Come on."

"Let's get to work, first," I said. "Sun's not getting any higher."

He liked this, of course, and so we went back outside to get some real work done. It had been a while since I'd had to really do manual labour, or at least what I considered manual labour. There were the usual chores around my mountaintop, but generally speaking the less I did for it, the better for me in terms of keeping out unwanted visitors.

The work he had me doing was good, old fashioned manual labour; he had me trim the grass and weeds around the house, just keeping it in better general condition here and there. It was the simplest, least important work that probably most people ignored usually, but since I'd shown up and had volunteered, it was a perfect job for me.

They were keeping their farm in top condition, in every possible way. They rotated crops, of course, and almost every spare inch of land was used to grow food or flowers or herbs; it was always being kept. There were no stray parcels of "boonies", it was all being used and kept. This was a place of life. This place produced things to keep us all alive.

The farm had a number of dogs and cats and a few other domesticated animals. They, too, were well kept and cared for. Off on the horizon, I could see that they were building a second farmhouse or barn or something.

When the sun started going down so low that work became impractical, all the workers put away their tools and supplies, and started meandering inside, gathering indoors.

The interiour of the house was well lit from the solar batteries, and some group of cooks had prepared a meal the likes of which I hadn't had in as far back as I could remember. Fresh food, cooked with pride, presented like it was a painting or a sculpture.

Before the revolution, there were three kinds of food. First there was the poison they fed the poor, and then there was the flavourless-but-functional "local cuisine" that most everyone ate from time to time simply to survive, and finally there was the "gourmet" which was, I believe, a foreign word, and ended up being contrived, overly-theatrical food that only the Rich got to eat and generally convinced themselves was something special and significant. All three had all but killed the societies "living" off of them.

There was still functional food. It was what I'd lived off of for the past four years probably. But the other kind of food was art food. It was food that people who loved to cook made for everyone. That was their way of contributing to a town project or a farm project. They cooked. They made meals. They gave you a meal that you looked at, and didn't want to eat because it was so beautiful. Make no mistake, it might not be elaborate, but there was humanity to it, and you can always tell when food is sincere. And when you eat it with your neighbours and comrades, you are participating in someone else's project, a cooking project designed to raise the esteem and very consciousness of the general population. They were militantly dedicated chefs who would only serve food they were proud of, to either man or beast. Even the dogs ate well. Because when you have nothing better to do with your time, that's what you do, and everyone in the world appreciates it.

Good food, healthy food, artistic food, was saving this planet. Right along with the destruction of the cities and the abolishing of ownership and everything the Revolution had implemented.

During dinner, I got to speak to more people. They were all curious as to where I was from and why I was traveling. I told them some stories.

"I was living in KBV," I said. "Our radio receiver blew out, or something, and so eventually I talked to the local commie and asked if there was something I could do to help, and so he gave me some parts and told me if I found anyone who could fix 'em, he might be able to fix it."

"Who's the commie over in KBV?" someone asked.

It was a truth test, I knew. So I said, "Gunther...Gunther something. Gunther Wilkes?"

"You mean Gunther Wilson," the girl who'd asked me said.

"Yeah, I think you're right about that. Wilson."

Now, I'd talked to Gunther Wilson every day for the past two years. His username was gwilson. Heck, I knew his name. But I didn't want them to all know I was a commie. Commies don't self-identify, in real life. Few people can say they've met a commie, because we never tell people that we are a commie. There's no pressing reason for it, it's not that we're ashamed or afraid or shy. But the tenet of never volunteering information, that's something commies live by.

Which is also why when everyone kept referring to me as a man, I didn't correct them.

"I kin take a look at the broken parts you got," the girl said, obviously the handyman my host had mentioned to me before.

"After dinner," I said, "OK."

"Did you used to be a chef over in KBV?" a muscular fellow sitting not far from me asked.

"Nope."

"How 'bout a tech?"

"I did some tech work," I said, "Just fixin' stuff. Random stuff, electric mostly."

"Then how come you can't fix the radio for your commie?" someone else asked.

"I'm not an electrical engineer, just good with wiring and current," I said.

The meathead was still staring at me, trying to place me from KBV as either a chef or a tech. I didn't like it but I didn't show it. He finally said, "I'd swear I know you from someplace."

"Well, I don't know you." And it was true. I didn't.

Chapter 8. Night on the Farm

After dinner was over and everyone had more or less warmed up to me, I grabbed the circuit board with a bad strip on it from my backpack and brought it to the handyman. She examined it and saw the bad strip and shrugged, saying, "Could probably bridge it."

"That hard?" I asked.

"It ain't impossible," she said, "But it ain't necessarily easy neither. Plus, depends on if you got spare strips."

"You got any?"

She pondered it for a few moments, pretending to examine the board itself. There wasn't really any reason to examine the board, they're all pretty much the same. So she obviously had some, or the answer would have been immediate, but I knew she was really deciding whether she wanted to give up one of her spare parts to me. I liked her. She was a little like a commie. Rough around the edges, maybe, but smart enough not to jump into something she might regret later on.

"No," she said at last. "I ain't got any strips, and I can't figure anything to substitute for it right now, so..." she shrugged and handed me the board back. "You'd be best off hanging onto that til you find someone with konsole parts."

"OK, thanks," I said, and went back to the bunk room.

I put the board back in my backpack and crawled up into my rack. It was comfortable enough, so I lay there, thinking about why no-one had yet mentioned that they hadn't received any transmissions. Possibly they didn't listen to the daily broadcasts, but more likely they did. Maybe they just didn't really care and assumed that the transmissions would be back when they were back.

One of the men in the room, reading an old science fiction novel, put down his book and said, "We have showers if you want."

"OK," I said. I thought about it a moment, and then said, "Maybe. Where are they?"

"Down the hall," he said. "Come on I'll show you."

I followed him down the main hallway, passing the other bunk rooms, a workshop and a supply room, and then we came to an extension that had been added to the shower, right where the back porch probably had been a long time ago, with rocking chairs and a porch table. Now it was two shower rooms, one for the men and one for the women. We might bunk together, but getting naked in front of each other still hadn't quite been worked out yet. The Children of Elektronix had tried it for a while. It didn't really work. We made it work, but it was fake. Something having to do with biology, I guess.

He opened the door to the men's shower room and, well, sure enough there were about eight men all standing at open stalls, showering. Men didn't use shower curtains for some reason, that's one thing I've noticed about a lot of men's showers, from what my male friends have told me. I don't really know why. I've always assumed it was a suppressed male need to be looked at, to be seen naked, to have their bodies appreciated. For a very long time, the classic "phallic" symbol was always supposed to have been an icon of power and strength. But at the same time, men's bodies were very taboo, and instead it was the female form that society plastered everywhere in various states of undress. I think men got jealous about that, and wanted people to look at them and think they were beautiful, too. So they look at each other's bodies, and appreciate each other silently.

Now nobody gets their naked body plastered anywhere. We don't need to do that. We don't have toothpaste to sell, or cars to sell, or clothes to market. We just have what we need, and we don't need a near-naked woman telling us to go purchase it.

I stood looking pensively at the naked men, admiring for a few moments their bodies and their deliberate movement. There was one man, in the farthest shower stall, and his movements were smooth and graceful. I figured he was probably a chef or a artisan of some sort, but I was making assumptions. He could have been the best harvester in the room, for all I knew.

People were interesting to watch. I hadn't seen people in a very long time, much less a room full of naked men. The longer I stood and watched, the more the fact that I hadn't been around a man in a long time was starting to nag at me, so I finally turned back, saying, "Well, I'll go in later when it's emptier. Looks like they're all taken now."

"Yeah, any time," the sci fi reader said. "People generally try to keep it under 5 minutes so the turn-around is good."

I noticed a mirror at the end of the room. I hadn't actually seen myself in a few days. I told the reader, "I'll hang out here, see if one frees up any time soon. Thanks."

He nodded and departed, and I continued on toward the mirror. I wanted to see why everyone thought I was a man. It was a full mirror, which was something I hadn't had, maybe ever. So I stood in front of it and looked.

The person I saw was a little weary and dirty. Unkempt and, heck, let's face it, probably smelly. I didn't look like a man, though, not really. Just a little androgynous due to a few understated features here and there that might've made it easier to peg me for a female. So I wasn't the most effeminate female on the planet. I didn't care. I kept a habit of cutting my hair as low as I could, just for convenience sake. It was a habit I'd gotten from the Children of Elektronix, where we'd all shaved our heads and kept them shaved. I'd gotten a lot of good bad-habits from that group.

I think more than anything, everyone was now assuming I was a man because the first fellow who'd seen me had thought I was a man as I approached, and I never said otherwise, so now I was a man to everyone there. And since it didn't really matter one way or another, I guess nobody was going to bother to clarify.

When the men's shower room cleared out, I decided to risk a quick shower. So I went into the men's shower and took the back-most stall, undressing there, and starting the water. They had warm water, sun-heated probably. Simple enough. I took what must have been a good eight minutes to shower; I needed it. I was filthy. I think I must have gone through an entire bar of soap scrubbing myself down.

As luck would have it, only one man came in during the shower, but I kept my back to him and for the most part he didn't really notice me, until, I think, his shower was over and I was still scrubbing myself down. I could hear him dressing, over by the door, and he said, "That's a nasty scar you got."

"Yep."

And that was that. I did have a scar. Last I checked, it went down the left side of my back pretty much from my shoulder all the way down to my left buttock. Four inches to the right and I'd probably have no spine today.

After I finally got clean, I walked back toward the bunks. On the way, I noticed the handyman in the little workshop, and stopped. I stood in the doorway and she noticed me fairly quickly.

"Whut."

"No daily broadcasts here? Sounds like maybe you got radio issues yourself?" I said.

"Radio's workin'," she said. "Broadcasts ain't."

"We were getting the them in KBV," I said.

"How long ago did you leave? Must've been at least 5 days ago unless you walk a lot faster than it looks like you could."

I thought a little, then said, "'Bout nine days ago, I guess."

"Yeah, that's 'bout when the broadcasts stopped comin' in."

"I guess the broadcast tower must be out," I said.

"Nope," she said. "I picked up another tower on shortwave, so if the tower was out, they'd have announced it, first of all, and second of all they'd've asked for handyman assistance until it got un-broke."

Yes, I liked this girl. She knew what she was talking about. That's why she was the handyman.

"You got a name?" I asked.

"Nope."

"OK. Wellp, good night."

"Night."

Chapter 9. The Journey Continues

> When a comrade is in danger and the question
> arises whether this comrade should be saved
> or not saved, the decision must not be arrived
> at on the basis of sentiment, but solely in the
> interests of the revolutionary cause. Therefore,
> it is necessary to weigh carefully the usefulness
> of the comrade against the expenditure of
> revolutionary forces necessary to save the
> comrade, and the decision must be made
> accordingly.
> — The Revolutionary's Catechism

The next morning I ate breakfast with the farmers, which I appreciated since I wasn't actually staying around to do any work that day, which they knew and still invited me to stay and eat. So we ate breakfast, and they all gave me travel tips, including the fastest way to get to KCG, and also that cranks had been rumoured to be out and about on the main road between here and KCG, so I might want to stick to one of the side routes.

"It'll be more like a hike that way, rather than a Sunday stroll, but I reckon it'd be safer," said the reader.

"I heard 'bout some cranks up near WKV or someplace," I said, "But I ain't heard of cranks round here yet."

"A transport from KCG passed by here, day before yesterday," he said. "That's where we heard about it."

"Any shots fired?" I asked.

"Yes," the reader said.

"No," my host said.

"Maybe," someone else said.

"Depends on who in the transport you asked," the reader explained. "Some people said they definitely heard a few shots. Other people didn't hear nothin."

"What kinda cranks would they have been if they couldn't hit the broad side of a transport?" my host said. "They either wasn't cranks, or they didn't take a shot."

It seemed logical to me.

"Stranger things have happened," the reader said.

That also seemed logical to me.

After breakfast, I thanked everyone for their hospitality and got back on the road.

Down by the road, just as I was leaving the property, the meathead from the previous night, was conveniently mending the fence which, naturally, didn't really look like it needed mending. As I passed, he stopped working and said, "You know where I swear I seen you?"

"Nope," I said and kept walking.

"KNY," he said, walking along the other side of the fence to keep up with me.

"Yeah, I been there," I said. "Not much, but I been there."

"I think you was with a group there. One of them militia groups, you know what I mean?"

"'Fraid I wasn't around for the militia," I said, assuming that he meant The Militia, which was the term most people used for the People during the time of the Revolution.

"Well it was more of a subgroup," he conceded. "Maybe you heard of 'em. Children of Elektronix."

"Sounds familiar," I said. "Yeah, sounds very familiar. Something about destroying remnants of the old world?"

"Yeah," he said. "That was them. You're walkin' pretty fast. You in a hurry?"

"Yes I am," I said, looking straight at him. "I told you I'm trying to get parts fixed for KBV. As long as it takes me, that's how long they don't get the broadcasts."

"Funny, we're not gettin' broadcasts either at this point. Feels like some subgroup might be up to their old tricks. Maybe the Children of Elektronix decided the radio stations were a little too Old World for them?"

"I don't know," I said and laughed. "Might wanna ask around about that, though, thanks. Don't work too hard."

And with that, I was past the fence. I was hoping he wouldn't hop over the fence and follow me down the road until he finally tired of interrogating me. Happily, he did not bother, but I could sense his eyes on me for quite a while as I walked on down the road.

Continuing my journey, I felt refreshed from my stay on the farm but no further enlightened. It sounded as if the tower thought it was sending out transmissions, or else they had stopped sending transmission intentionally. No call for help had been issued, yet obviously broadcasts were not being received. There was definitely a breach in logic there. Could be that their commie had passed into the great Dev Null, and maybe nobody else there knew how to send messages, in which case they probably had dispatched someone on foot to go find a new commie. But I knew the commies, and I knew the commie over in KCG well enough to know that he'd have had an apprentice to cover his job if anything bad happened to him. So I didn't think that was it.

Whatever it was, things weren't quite adding up, and I was starting to wonder if just walking into KCG and asking them to please fix their tower was really all it was going to take to fix the issue.

The only alternative was to go back to the mountaintop, though, and try to pick up someone else's signal on shortwave, boost that, and re-transmit. But that is what they know as treating the symptom and not the disease, and it wasn't the Children of Elektronix way.

Damn revolutionaries. Spend your formative years around those sorts, and you start picking up the best habits that you'll never be able to shake. The Children of Elektronix didn't settle for quick fixes. They didn't settle for patching up a symptom without attacking the disease. They wouldn't have sent a konsole message and then throw up their hands when nothing happened, saying, "I've done everything I can."

They were about taking what they called "direct action". Identify the problem, and take whatever action is required to directly affect that problem until it is fixed. Don't launch a campaign to work around the problem, don't launch an awareness group to gather a large team of a useless majority. Just do what needs to be done.

It was not something you can leave behind once you've done it long enough. And when, after such a mission to take action against a particularly large problem, you're lying on the ground with a gash down your back that nearly sliced a third of your body clean off the rest of you, and these hard-headed, self-important, overly-philosophic people save your life in spite of the resources it takes to do so, then like the scar that the cut left, their principles are embedded within you forever.

And so, I was taking direct action, one way or another.

I stuck to the side "road" as advised by my hosts. They were right to say that it was a different walk, entirely; the side road was more of a path, higher up than the main road itself, and far less maintained. I could tell it was used from time to time, although I couldn't imagine for what. I guess it was used by people like me, who didn't want to be seen on the main road for one reason or another, although it didn't seem there was a lot of traffic on the main road, either.

Just a little bit after the sun reached its highest point, I did notice a few large vans down on the main road. I'd almost missed them at first, they were fairly well camouflaged against the dark-ish earthtones surrounding the main road, but there were people there and I usually noticed people no matter what.

I stopped walking to watch. It seemed like there were too many people there, just a little bit too much activity around the vans than what there should have been. They had a tire and some tools out by one of the vans, and a blanket on the ground. But they weren't working on anything. They weren't changing a tyre or fixing the van, they were just mulling about, aimlessly. It didn't make sense to me, but I got the distinct sense that these were cranks. They didn't look like the stereotypical cranks, whatever that looked like. Mean, I guess. They looked nice enough, but they looked like they were also fake. Like they were trying to look nice.

They didn't all have guns, but some of them did. And they were formidable guns. I figured they were probably on the lookout for passers-by. Whenever someone did pass, they all set about to working, like one of the vans had broken down. They'd flag down a transport or some group passing by, ostensibly for help. And then they take everything worth anything, at gunpoint, and who knows what they do with the humans attached to it all.

I was brought out of my thoughtful observance by the sound of approaching feet. It startled me to the quick, and my heart began to race. I hadn't felt that degree of fear and excitement in a long while, and I didn't much care for it now. My eyes widened to twice their usual size, my ears were open, hair on the back of my neck was standing up straight, I was like a wild animal. It wasn't something I could control, and I could taste adrenaline in my mouth.

I looked down and saw that I was holding my Springfield. I didn't remember taking it off my back, but there it was in my hands, ready to break someone's nose, or put an extra hole through their head if necessary.

But I was backing up, off the path, into the bank, behind trees, behind the brush. And I was crouching down and taking aim at the road, but keeping my head on a swivel and my ears perked up. I was ready for whatever was coming, and there just wasn't any way around that.

I could hear the footsteps getting closer, but it was from sunset direction, up the path toward me. That seemed like the wrong direction for a crank to be coming; they'd be coming up the mountain side, or possibly from a low point that I hadn't reached yet further toward the sunrise. But not all the way from sunset. Still, I watched and listened.

Finally, the figure appeared up over the ridge. I couldn't make out who or what it was, but I did notice that if it had a gun then it wasn't a rifle, and it wasn't drawn.

When it got closer, I could see who it was. It was the handyman, from the farm. She indeed did not have a gun drawn, but she was moving carefully and seemed alert. It seemed like she knew that the cranks were below. I wondered what she was up to, and whether or not she was looking for me on this path, or whether she was looking to see if I'd gone back down to the cranks, like I was one of them, and had only gone to the farm to scout it out for a raid. I didn't blame them.

In fact, I'd have probably done the same thing if someone had wandered up to my mountaintop.

Then again, maybe the meathead had gotten her interested and suspicious of me for entirely different reasons. I don't know exactly what anyone on GPL farmlands would have with a former Children of Elektronix member, but everyone has disagreements and differences over something. I certainly didn't much care for the meathead's tone when he'd been talking to me.

I couldn't get to the handyman now, not without scaring her half out of her wits the way she did me. And if she had a gun it probably would be drawn at that point and one of us would end up getting shot, or else we'd just make a lot of noise and then we'd both be in trouble with the cranks. So I sat up on the hillside, resting against the tree that concealed me, watching the handyman watch the cranks. She had a sniper scope with her, only without a sniper attached, and she was using it as a telescope to get a better look at what was going on.

When she was satisfied with whatever she was curious about, she put the scope away and moved on. She kept going in the sunrise direction, which struck me as odd. I'd expected her to turn back and return to the farm. So either my assumption that she was scouting the cranks for any sign of me there was wrong or else she had a secondary agenda.

Once she was more or less out of earshot, I descended again, this time following her. I had no desire to follow her in secret, but did so until we ourselves were well away from the cranks below. Once I felt we were distant enough to be able to safely speak, I quickened my pace and, as I'd hoped she would, she heard me approach and turned to look. When she saw it was she me, she looked both relieved but also substantially suspicious.

"Where did you just come from?" she asked.

"Why are you following me?"

"Followin' you? how was I 'sposed to know you were on the highroad, and it seems like you're followin' me."

"Your friends told me to take this road," I said. "So what were you doing back there looking at that group down on the road?"

That clearly took her by surprise, the realization that she'd been watched without her knowledge. Obviously if I'd been a crank, or else if I was in collaboration with the cranks as they probably had sent her to find out, she'd have been captured, or worse.

She repositioned herself a little, physically to mirror the glaringly obvious mental shift I'd just caused. "OK, so we were a little curious about whether or not you knew anything about them cranks. Just wondering if there was any connection, you know."

"Thought so," I said. "Don't blame you, I'd have checked myself in your place."

We stood in silence for a few moments, processing, I think, whether we had any distrust remaining or if everything could be as simple as it seemed. I didn't quite believe her about why she'd been following me, still thinking of that meathead inquisition, but for the time being, I trusted her, I decided. The farmers had been good people, so I saw nothing out of the ordinary with them verifying that I was as innocent as I seemed. Whoever it was who'd seen the scar on my back had probably reported that, too. Anybody can have a scar, but when a suspicious stranger has a gash down their back and doesn't provide a friendly explanation and claims to be a simple technician, anyone would start to wonder.

I could tell she didn't distrust me, either. She seemed like a pretty good judge of people, and I wondered if she'd agreed to do this reconnaissance mission more because it had to be done than because she thought it was valid.

She looked me over with a quick movement of her eye, and I knew she knew I was not a man, but was perhaps unclear as to whether I myself knew it. Commies didn't volunteer information, so I didn't say anything.

She said at last, "I'm going someplace in the same direction as the way you're going. Mind if we travel together?"

"I don't mind."

"Seems like you know how to take care of yourself," she said.

"Yep."

We walked.

Chapter 10. Travel Partners

> The sixth category is especially important: women. They can be divided into three main groups. First, those frivolous, thoughtless, and vapid women, whom we shall use as we use the third and fourth category of men. Second, women who are ardent, capable, and devoted, but whom do not belong to us because they have not yet achieved a passionless and austere revolutionary understanding; these must be used like the men of the fifth category. Finally, there are the women who are completely on our side – i.e., those who are wholly dedicated and who have accepted our program in its entirety. We should regard these women as the most valuable or our treasures; without their help, we would never succeed.
>
> — The Revolutionary's Catechism

For a while, we walked in silence, maybe still trying to distance ourselves from the cranks, maybe trying to decide what topic to breach first. It was probably the former, because when the handyman did speak, it was about the scam going on below:

"That's the new thing, I've heard; they pretend to have a borked vehicle, they flag someone down for help, and that's the end of that. Now to add to the desperation, they have someone 'passed out' or having a heat stroke. They had a blanket on the ground for that."

"Yeah, I saw. I wondered what the blanket was for," I said.

"All part of the show," she said. "I never seen it done, thankfully, but I heard about it."

"So they thought I was a crank?" I said, of her farmer friends.

"I admit it crossed our minds," she said. "Figured you might be a scout or somethin'. Checking us out for supplies and weapons."

"Not like cranks to take on an established facility, is it?" I said. I'd been out of touch, but not that out of touch. If the situation had gotten as bad as that, I'd have heard it in the broadcasts.

"Never can be too careful," she said.

"Then how come they sent you out alone? You militia?" I asked this last question as a private joke for myself. I knew she wasn't militia, given that I'd watched her from 2 meters away for the better part of a quarter of an hour. But I also wanted to see if she'd give any indication of having talked to meathead.

"I insisted going alone," she said. "I have some business of my own to take care of."

"OK."

"How'd you get that scar?"

"What scar."

"The scar down the left side of your back. Bill told us about it. I told them accidents happen, but they seemed convinced it had been an injury in some violent confrontation."

"Bill told you about a scar?" I said.

"He said you had a scar down the left side of your back, clear from your shoulder on down to your ass."

"I'm afraid he mistook me for someone else," I said. "I don't have no scars."

She was quiet. We walked for a ways and I could feel the seething disbelief in her, building up new pressure, more questions.

I assessed what I knew about her, and what I was assuming about her. I assumed she was really a handyman, although I never saw her in action so I couldn't verify that. Some people are very good at passing themselves off as one thing or another without actually ever doing much of anything. I didn't know how long she'd been at the farm, maybe she was coasting on their good faith. Maybe she'd been coasting for a while, or maybe she was brand new there. A commie doesn't make assumptions.

I'd seen people claim to be competent at something for months and everyone would take them at their word. And when something needed done, their "expert" opinion would be that it couldn't be done, and people believed them. And sometimes, if they move on before any real issues require their attention, they could remain an expert on a subject they knew nothing about. I've seen it done.

Men had a tradition, long ago, called "shaking hands". Lots of silly ideas of how the tradition got started; some said that it was a literal sign that they weren't carrying a weapon (because apparently the idea of carrying a weapon in your left hand didn't occur to anyone), others claim that it was simply a nice way to acknowledge another person by using physical contact, and still others claim that the firmness of the grip and shake was a machismo indicator used to size up a potential opponent. I tend to believe that it was an old tradition that no one uses any more anyway, but it was once used, apparently.

It was, back when it was used, a probably accidental signature of complete trust. When two people met and shook hands, there was an instant kind of familiarity and trust instilled in each person. The two men were friends, even though they'd just met; they were friends because they had shaken hands, but really, it was because they'd touched. They'd made human contact.

I hadn't made human contact in a very long time.

It had been a man's ritual, the shaking of hands. You didn't find that many women who chose to partake in it, and women weren't ever expected to necessarily do so, and so few bothered. But for men, after they'd evaluated each other's handshake, they would start talking about anything on their mind. They might be complete strangers, but after the handshake, they would tell each other about everything they ever did.

Dexter, a commie across continent, said once that he missed the old handshaking days. He said for a commie, that was the best weapon of all. He said he'd go up to any man in a room, shake hands, and by the end of the evening he would have any information he needed from that man. It was just that easy.

Now, of course, no one shakes hands, and so the commies have, according to Dexter, lost their best weapon.

But there were similar weapons floating around. Similar ideas of gaining trust and then gaining information without ever surrendering any real information.

Some would ask me "Why did you lie about the scar on your back?"

Those people know nothing about information. If knowledge is power, then information is its currency. A commie knows this because all a commie does is deal with information, day in and day out. We receive it on our konsoles, we classify it, we organize it, we make correlations between them and then we classify the correlations we've made. And then finally we archive it. And people give it to us for free, at least twice a day.

This is how I knew that cranks, for example, were not responsible for the radio silence. I knew what cranks had been spotted where, and where they traveled from, and where they were probably traveling to. I know what towns are selling off surplus energy, which towns are hoarding food, which towns are growing, which ones are being abandoned. There is not much I didn't know, about the big picture of things going on in the world.

Disinformation is as valuable for an information collector as is real information. Telling the handyman that I had no scar on my back could have many results. Which one it might actually have, I did not know. I had no preference, but the revelation of the truth - confirming that I did have a scar - would only have one result: the handyman would know that I had a scar on my back. Not much more good could come from that. But from the disinformation, you just never really knew.

Chapter 11. Handyman

All revolutionaries should have under them second- or third-degree revolutionaries – i.e., comrades who are not completely initiated. these should be regarded as part of the common revolutionary capital placed at his disposal. This capital should, of course, be spent as economically as possible in order to derive from it the greatest possible profit. The real revolutionary is as capital consecrated to the triumph of the revolution; however, the revolutionary may not personally and alone dispose of that capital without the unanimous consent of the fully initiated comrades.

— The Revolutionary's Catechism

That night we set up camp together along the side of the road, first level clearing we found. We made a campfire for light, and the handyman brought forth a self-powered radio. I'd never seen anyone carry around one of those radios except commies, and a few handymen. That was, at least, a good sign.

She cranked the radio for a few minutes, and then started tuning it. She was careful in her tuning, slow and methodical. Not like most people non-techs, who spun the dial until they hit the loudest signal and then fiddled clumsily until they hit some sweet spot where there was discernible speech. A tech -- well, really a commie -- wanted all noise. They wanted to sample everything. They wanted static, they wanted dead air, they wanted faint signals, they wanted the closest broadcast, they wanted it all. And most of all, of course, they wanted Godstream.

And that's more or less what she did. She must have had a commie-like appreciation for radio. Who could say? maybe she was a commie. She wouldn't have announced it, and she wouldn't say if she was, if I asked. You can never tell.

"No signal?" I asked. It was a vulgar question, asked while she was listening to some of the most beautifully arrhythmic static I'd ever heard.

She ignored me for a few moments, just long enough to show that my commentary was not appreciated, and then she said, "Quite the contrary, there's signal all around us. Maybe not the signal you're looking for, but..."

"You a commie or something?" I asked.

"Are you?"

"Yeah."

She laughed. "OK, what's this?"

She spun the dial arbitrarily and it landed on the Godstream.

I jumped up, all but unable to conceal my surprise. I'd seen her spin the dial. It had been an uncalculated move. She hadn't even looked at the frequencies before doing it. And for it to have landed on the Godstream, after such a question. It was not natural. In fact it was the very definition of supernatural.

She stood and looked at me, hard. "What's wrong?"

"Turn that down," I said, still unsure if I could conceal the true reason for my reaction or not. "It hurts my ears."

"What does?"

"All that static," I said. "Can't you hear that high pitch in it?"

"What high pitch?" she asked. "I'm pitch perfect, I don't hear anything."

"Well I do, so turn it down please," I said.

She turned the volume down. I took my seat again. "I don't like all that noise. It sounds bad, and it's too loud."

"Well what do you think it is?" she asked.

"I don't think. I know." I was feeling more confident in my cover story now. "It's static. White noise."

"That's not white noise. White noise is all possible frequencies combined. This is noise. It's radio noise. But where do you think it's from?"

"I guess from a far off radio tower," I said, opening some food for myself. "We're out of range but we're getting little bits of their transmission here and there."

"I don't think so," she said. "I've listened to it. A lot. And there are little snippets in there that don't come from no radio tower I kin think of."

"Well, somebody's obviously broadcasting it," I said.

"Exactly. But who?" she said. I offered her some food, and she took the can from me and wolfed some down. She gave it back to me and continued, "My theory? whoever is broadcasting that, is interfering with our local tower."

I chuckled to myself at the idea of the Godstream being broadcast by some bored human being in an abandoned radio tower. "Doesn't sound quite powerful enough to interfere with any signal, to me."

"Maybe that's what they want you to think," she said.

"Well, it's hard to argue against that logic," I said, "if everything discounting the idea is just part of Their Brilliant Plan."

The radio's distorted and broken signal started to fade as it ran out of power. She didn't bother winding it again.

She was obviously a techie, I could see that now. And a thinker; I liked that. As misguided as some of her ideas might have been, at least she was thinking about the problems presented to her.

And she had an appreciation for signal, and the Godstream. And you don't have that and not impress a commie.

The campfire had died down, and the moon became concealed by clouds making it too dark to see even a hint of one another or our surroundings. It was peaceful.

I heard her voice in the darkness, hesitant and unsure of itself. She said: "There's a tower just sunrise and up a ways of KCG. It's in this mountain, kinda off from view but...at certain angles you can see it."

"What's its ID?" I asked.

"I don't know. I don't think it has one."

"Pirate radio?" I asked. "With a full tower?"

She shrugged, but I could tell she believed it. Firmly.

"Well if that's the case then what are they broadcasting? We'd pick that up instead of KCG, so we'd know about them one way or another."

"I think they're broadcasting static," she said. "Just to kill the KCG signal."

I considered this for a few moments. As bizarre as it seemed, it was a possibility. I couldn't think of a motive, but it was entirely possible. Overpower KCG's signal with a stronger signal of static, and suddenly there's no KCG for anyone.

"The commie in KCG would have heard about that," I said. "They have safeguards set in place for that sort of thing."

"Maybe that signal's blocking messages going in, as well."

"Then the commie in KCG would wonder why his entire world had disappeared, and he'd go around asking questions."

"Well maybe he's doin' just that, right now," she said.

"I hope not," I said. "If he is then we'll miss him in KCG and this trip will have been a big waste of time."

We laid down on the ground, my head on my backpack, and pretended to be tired. Well, I didn't have to entirely pretend, but I didn't intend to sleep yet. She took the queue, though, and also leaned against her backpack, looking up at the night sky. I watched her as the moon peeked out from behind the clouds. She was holding her radio in her hands.

"Where'd you learn to fix stuff?" I asked.

"My pa," she said. "Ain't that how everybody learns?"

"Not me," I said, "I learned from an old boyfriend."

That was actually more or less true.

"I coulda fixed your circuit board," she confessed. "Sorry I didn't."

"I thought maybe you coulda," I said. "But I understood. I don't know if I'd've given up a rare supply like that for a stranger, either."

She nodded, smiling at the comradeship of mutually recognized tech ethics. "Well, when we get back, I'll fix it if you want."

"What, that old thing?" I asked and laughed a little. "That's just a board I carry around for fun. It didn't really come out of KBV's radio."

She looked over at me in surprise. It often, in turn, surprised me at how many people accept everything anyone tells them, and then are so shocked to find out that something had been untrue, or exaggerated.

"It's a backup part," I lied further. "So it should get fixed at some point, but I don't want to take any of your spare parts for it. I'll find another board somewhere in a ditch and strip it for parts."

"Find a circuit board in a ditch?" she asked incredulously. "Where are you from that you find circuit boards just lying around in ditches?"

I shrugged. "You never know."

We lay in silence for a while, then her voice came again, doing what everyone does when they're laying in silence near still-warm embers, feeling secure with someone: talk about themselves. "I'm probably not goin' back to the farm. I'm thinkin' of goin' to KCG and getting in with their commie. Learn the trade, once and for all. Maybe settle in KCG, take over the commie's job when he moves on or dies."

She meant, of course, pass on to the great Dev Null. But she knew nothing of the Dev Null yet, and she wouldn't for a long time.

"That's as good a plan as any, I guess," I said. "You can definitely fix stuff, and you've got your own radio."

"That's not what commies do," she said. "A lotta people think that's all a commie is; someone who fixes radios and presses some magical button that makes all the broadcasts go. But, it's not like that."

"What do they do then," I said politely, pretending to be more tired than interested.

"Techies fix the radios," she said, "you know, handymen like me. Commies, now they deal with the actual broadcasts themselves. They receive them, and concatenate all the different streams into one, and then send it back out. Or something like that. You know, broadcasts are compiled. They don't just come from one place. All the towers send out the information, and all the other towers get each other's information, and they combine all that information into one broadcast. And then they play that for the local area. That's what you and I hear every day."

"I didn't know that," I said. "I thought it all came from the KCG tower."

"How would KCG know what was goin' on in KTN unless KTN told 'em?" she said. "It's not easy, that kind of work. It's a lot of information, and you have to know how to use the konsoles, and you have to archive all the old broadcasts, and if an emergency happens you have to know how to loop the announcement over and over again, all day, til its fixed."

"You sure know a lot about it," I said. She did know more than the average joe, but it was a rudimentary understanding. I admired her interest, though, and was doubly resolved not to let on that I myself was a commie. If she ever found that out, she wouldn't stop asking me questions about it, I could just hear her now.

"How long til KCG, do you reckon?" I asked.

"We'll get there tomorrow evening, I'd say. Well, maybe the next day, if we make any stops along the way."

"There are stops along the way?" I asked.

"There might be."

Chapter 12. Stash

> The nature of the true revolutionary excludes all sentimentality, romanticism, infatuation, and exaltation. All private hatred and revenge must also be excluded. Revolutionary passion, practiced at every moment of the day until it becomes a habit, is to be employed with cold calculation. At all times, and in all places, the revolutionary must obey not personal impulses, but only those which serve the cause of the revolution.
> — The Revolutionary's Catechism

In the morning, I awakened to find the handyman already awake and finishing up her breakfast. She was used to early mornings, having lived on a farm most recently. I stretched, and she offered me some water. I drank. She offered me food but I wasn't hungry.

We cleaned up the campsite, put out the fire, didn't bother leaving food because it was a rarely traveled road, and continued on our way.

The main road was empty, as was our private highroad. I suggested we move down to the main road for ease of travel but she protested, saying that she still felt uneasy about the cranks that had been spotted in the area. I reckoned they were going to be stationary for a while, with their broken down van scam, but she insisted we stay the course.

Sometimes you'll see things like that. Cranks who've been running the same scam for so long that they basically just set up camp along the road, and then they stay there for so long that the camp turns into an encampment, and they start to settle in so comfortably that the encampment becomes a shanty town, and it gets put on somebody's map at some point, and they're not considered cranks any more. Maybe an unfriendly shanty town, but not cranks. Sometimes they become legitimate traders just out of necessity.

But the handyman and I kept hiking along the highroad, just to keep away from trouble. It meant more hiking, which took greater effort at a slower rate, but the handyman was convinced it was for the best, and I was not presumptuous or foolish enough to believe I knew better than a local.

It wasn't long before, predictably, the main road started to veer away from the highroad we were on. I pointed this out to the handyman but she said we could take the highroad a little further before diverging ourselves, and that's when I started to get suspicious.

"This road is on a mountain," I said, "if we keep going, we'll end up circumambulating it and eventually we'll be going away from KCG."

"No, I know a shortcut," she said.

"What kind of shortcut?"

"It'll bridge a big curve that the main road makes and we'll save hours off the journey," she said.

I stopped walking and so she stopped too. I said, "And walk into what, exactly?"

"What do you mean?"

"The road goes that way," I said pensively, "and this path goes this way. I don't see how the two could ever merge further down this path."

"Not this path, but along the way," she said.

"And you," I was almost thinking aloud, "you came on what could have been a dangerous mission, all alone. Seems like that would be very non-threatening to me. Might make me lower my guard...so I'd be more vulnerable later on."

She looked surprised and a little confused. "Why would I want to ambush you?"

"Could be you're all cranks," I said, suddenly feeling like I was right. Like the whole world had been taken over by crooks and pirates and opportunists. "Maybe you think I'm someone important, or you think I could be of some value to you."

She was silent for a long while, processing my theory. It struck me that she was sincerely perplexed at the idea, which comforted me a little.

"I'm not taking you on a shortcut," she finally admitted. "But I'm not leadin' you into no ambush either. There's a safe haven, not far from where we are now. I'm the only one who knows about it. On the entire planet, I'm the only one. I was going to take you to it."

"Why?"

"Because I know you're up to somethin'," she said. "I couldn't understand why everyone was callin' you a man back at the farm, first of all, and why you never corrected nobody. I figured since you'd been seen in the male showers you must really think you are a male. OK, no problem. But the scar? and the way you reacted to the radio static? now that was interesting. You're up to somethin', and whatever it is, I wanna be up to it, too."

There was no point in standing around and talking, so I resumed walking, letting her lead the way.

She continued: "I understand you ain't gonna let me in on whatever secret you're in on without a little collateral, so I figure I may as well show you what I got. Then maybe you'll tell me a little about what you know."

"What do you think I know?" I asked.

"I think there's a commie revolution going on," she said. "I think the commies have banded together and are takin' over."

"What's there to take over?" I asked. "They already run the infrastructure of all the communication in the world. Seems t'me they took over from day one."

I said this because it is truly what I believed. The commies had taken over a long, long time ago, probably even before the Revolution and before they were even called commies.

"Well then they're working on somethin' big," she said. "I don't know what it is, but KCG going silent has something to do with it."

"You've got as much an imagination as I have," I said. "KCG going silent is due to the fact that KCG has gone silent. Probably their commie fell down a mountainside and now nobody can figure out how to op the konsole. Maybe that'll be your job."

"I ain't even seen a konsole much less op one," she said. "Besides, KCG's commie would have had an apprentice. They always do."

I hadn't had an apprentice. If I'd fallen off my perch, some commie would have had to notice that I wasn't sending out my broadcasts, and eventually someone would have to go, on foot, to investigate. Thinking of this, I saw that it had been a glaring oversight that I'd basically managed to repress for too long.

But what had really struck me about what the handyman had said was the legends that were clearly building up around the commies. "They always have an apprentice"? It sounded like it was common knowledge. Like commies literally never deviated from some kind of unwritten law, like they weren't human and so never were different from one another in any way. All commies were alike; they were, each and every one of them, calculated, methodical, perfect.

Like a naked man in the shower. Like anything you see for a few moments, and form a lifetime-full of stories about. They are perfect, without flaw. The are flawless and legendary. And completely foreign to you, but infinitely alluring.

Chapter 13. Some Food

The handyman and I walked for another hour, up the side of a mountain and somewhat behind it, until we reached what appeared to have been an abandoned town. It would have been a small town, maybe some kind of outpost. No buildings were actually standing but you could make out the outline of where there had been streets and foundations. Some of the road remained but mostly it was flat grassy land.

The handyman took a good look around us, and when she felt it was safe, she walked over to a pile of rubble near what had once been the foundation of a building, and started moving rocks and bricks from the area. I helped.

We'd soon uncovered a pair of metal doors. They were locked together with an old and hefty lock, which the handyman unlocked swiftly with a key she produced from a chain of a few keys and trinkets that she wore around her neck, concealed beneath her clothes.

She opened one of the doors and started down the stairs, and motioned for me to follow. She was motioning urgently, apparently truly afraid of being seen going into her secret lair. As for me, I was less concerned about who might be looking on as I was with who or what might be down in this secret bunker.

I didn't care about appearances. I drew my Springfield and held it by my side, and followed her down.

I could tell that she was nervous about the rifle, but I figured it was better her than me. I watched both the direction we were headed and the doors above us. But soon we'd descended enough so that the doors were no longer visible, and we were in darkness.

I could hear her moving about, presumably to find something to light the room. When she did turn on a light, it was a small but bright electric lantern she'd brought with her. Solar powered and very bright. I assumed she hadn't used it at the campsite due to the brightness, but down here we were safe from prying eyes and could enjoy as much light as necessary.

Once my eyes adjusted, I looked around the room carefully. There were crates and crates of MRE's -- that is, the prepackaged "Meals Ready-to-Eat" that the old world US Army and health services had distributed to soldiers and civilians alike. That was just before the Revolution. After the Revolution, the people had just taken all the MRE's they wanted because there was no such thing as a US Army any more.

There were trunks of dried fruit. Barrels of water. Medical supplies, ammunition, books, a myriad ESP's ("electronic spare parts"), a few random weapons, and some other supplies whose purposes were so obsolete now that probably neither of us could have identified.

It sickened me to see all of these supplies, hoarded, secreted away from the people to whom it all really belonged. The handyman had found this private desperate hoard of stuff, and instead of sharing it with everyone, she kept it all for herself. It was greed, through and through. It was the old dog-eat-dog model of the capitalists and opportunists.

I wanted to run up the stairs at that moment and swing wide the metal doors, and shout out into the air so everyone would hear me, that there was a stockpile of goods free for the taking.

At one time in my life, I'd have done it without hesitation. That was the time when I was a "child of the electronik age", a freedom fighter, a militant destroyer of the old ways and preserver of the new ideals. If that had meant the handyman's ostracization or even destruction, I'd have chalked that up to a necessary and acceptable loss.

But today I was different. The handyman hadn't been in the Children of Elektronix. She hadn't been taught all of the values I'd been taught, even though everyone should be taught those from birth. But it wasn't her fault that she hadn't gotten the lessons.

In fact, I reflected as I strolled around the room pretending to be reading the labels and looking at the supplies, it was my fault, ultimately. As a member of the Children of Elektronix I'd sworn to destroy the old models and reinforce the new ideals. And then I became a commie, and I claimed to organize and distribute information. The natural flow from one to the other was glaringly obvious, yet it hadn't happened. I was a split personality, or a single personality living a double life. I was both of these things; a militant and a commie, but never both in the same action.

Direct action. That is what I'd sworn I would take. And the most direct thing for a commie who was also an Elektrik Child was to broadcast the new ideas, the new values, the new ethics, far and wide.

To do that, I'd need more commies than just me doing it. Meaning I needed Children of Elektronix in commie positions. The Children of Elektronix needed to take over the commies, and the commies needed to have their own private revolution. Just as the handyman had theorized. Only much, much better.

I said, "This is enough for an entire army."

She nodded, not proudly or eagerly, just matter-of-factly. "I found it last year. I figure on moving out this way, maybe making a settlement right here, but, I couldn't do it alone."

"What about becoming a commie?" I asked. "I thought you said you want to do that."

"I do," she said. "Once I'm good enough, I could probably set up a tower right here, use this place as my broadcast center."

It was, I admitted, a good plan.

She started packing her mostly empty backpack with the various supplies she'd come for; some food, mostly electronic parts, some ammunition, some light medical supplies.

"If you need to re-stock," she said, "you're welcome to. As you can see, there's plenty here."

I took a few MRE's and put them into my bag. I found some ammo for my guns, and took a box, only because I didn't exactly see them lying around every day. I also went to the pile of electronic spare parts and fished around for a circuit board. There were a few small boards, dusty and probably useless, but if I stripped them for spare parts they could be given new life. I showed one to her questioningly and she nodded, giving me silent permission to take it.

"See? I toldja I'd find one."

She smiled and said, "That wasn't in a ditch."

"It was a turn of phrase."

"Wanna eat?" she said. "Might be nice to have a hot meal before moving on. We could stay here the night, if you're not in a hurry."

"I'm not in a hurry," I said. "Let's eat, and then move on. We're close to KCG?"

"We could make it another four hours maybe," she said. "We'll get there just before nightfall I'd bet, as long as we get back on the road soon."

The handyman boiled some water on a little gas stove there in the bunker, dropped the heatable bags of the MRE in, and we were soon eating hot stew and pasteurized cheese on stale crackers. It was good enough Traveling food, or at least better than cold beans from a can. The stew was beef, which repelled me. Used to be people ate animals all the time, three times daily in fact. So much so that factories were erected just to birth, and kill, animals. It was an endless cycle of life and death simply to serve the dietary whims of the dominant race. We didn't have factories now, so the only time people at meat was when they could catch an animal and manage to kill it, or if they raised animals themselves. I myself ate very little meat. mainly only when it existed from before the Revolution. To not eat that meat would be a waste of many things, including resources, the animal's life, and the toil and labour of the people who had killed and packaged the animal for consumption. I was not prepared to send all of that effort and suffering into the great Dev Null without it having had purpose.

After we ate, we refilled our canteens and went back above ground. She closed and locked the metal doors, and we placed rocks and rubble on the door. The effect in the end was that the platform leading into the bunker looked like the collapsed remains of a pillar or column, of no more interest than any of the rest of the debris in the area. I surveyed the area when we were finished.

"It could make a good radio station," I agreed with the handyman. "Maybe too low. You might have to move higher on the mountain. Keep this as a storage area."

She joined me in the survey, for the first time, I think, really paying attention to what her eyes were seeing. People, when they look out at the world, often imposes a kind of physics-less power to what they see. That's why they make misjudgments about distance or height; they'll say things like "that cliff isn't so high, I could jump into the river from there" -- and then once they are at the peak of the cliff, staring down into the water far below, they cower in fear.

But if you really pay attention to what your eye is seeing, you can get a lot of information. And so now when the handyman was emulating my deliberate gaze at the things around us, she was seeing things as a part of her surroundings, realizing that a broadcast from this very location would be blocked immediately by trees and the sister mountain not far away. There were great physical limitations around us that, in her minds eye, she'd been able to scale easily. But radio waves were limited by simple physics, and there wasn't really a way around that.

"I think you might be right," she said after a careful look around. "I hadn't noticed before but I'd get a lot of interference from here."

I shrugged. "Seems like it to me. But the mountain itself seems good. Close enough to the main road to have access, but recessed. I guess someone built this outpost here for some reason."

"I wonder how old it is," she said. "And what it was."

I didn't know enough about history to even hazard a guess, but I used my imagination. "A mountaineer outpost? for a mountain militia? or maybe a post office exchange."

"What's a post office exchange?"

"I don't know," I said, because I didn't, really.

At that moment, we both saw movement just over the nearest ridge. My hand went intellectually for my rifle, and I didn't let my brain intervene; my rifle was drawn and ready in moments. Neither of us seemed willing to investigate what we'd seen, at least not immediately, but I figured since we weren't being shot at yet then whatever we'd seen was relatively harmless, so I made the first move. The handyman followed and even started to overtake me, unarmed though she was.

We found, just over the little peak of the flatland, a man walking briskly away back toward the road. I took aim with my rifle and called after him, "Keep walking and you won't be walking for much longer."

He looked back casually, saw my rifle, stopped dead in his tracks. He put up his arms and turned slowly toward us.

"Come on back here," I called. The handyman waved her arms for him to return.

He didn't seem to like the sound of that, but obeyed nevertheless. The man was clearly a wanderer, or a mountain-man, unshaven, unwashed, and a little vacant in his eyes. The closer he got, the more powerful his stench became and the handyman's tolerance for that was low so she told him to stop before the stench overpowered us entirely.

"What are you doing 'round here?" I asked him. "You spying on us? Following us?"

"I ain't followin' y'all," he said. Most of his teeth were missing, and his voice was raspy and raw. "I never even seen y'all before."

"Well what're you doing on our mountain then?" I asked. I could feel the handyman watching me, I could almost hear her taking mental notes on what I was doing, how I was speaking to the man, the assertions I was making off the cuff. She was smart, so I knew she now knew I'd done this sort of thing once or twice before.

"I didn't know it was y'all's mountain," he said. He was strangely unafraid of the rifle, but he respected it. I felt distinctly unafraid of him but I held fast just in case.

"How long you been here spyin' on us?" I asked.

"I just got here, I seen y'all and I figgered on askin' if you had anything to spare, it's been a real hard winter up here in these parts'n whatnot. I been lookin' for somethin' to eat better part of the month and I ain't found nothin' but a few acorns."

"You eatin' acorns?" the handyman asked. "You know them're poisonous?"

"Well I gotta eat somethin'."

"Well this here's our mountain, we found it and we're startin' to build a radio tower on it, so if you wanna get shot, you come on up for a visit sometime. Otherwise, you stay off it and we'll get along just fine. There's gonna be twenty of us next week right here, you understand?"

"I understand, I was just lookin' fer some food and whatnot. I got no cause t' be up here anyway, I live back over there in the woods, got myself a real nice clearing where I stay, it's pretty nice and keeps clear of most people not that I don't like people but people don't tend to like me, or rather, they like t' tell me what I can and can't do which I'm not so fond of."

"Yeah, ok," I said. "Now git."

"Here, take this," the handyman said and threw an MRE to the man. He caught it and looked at it, puzzled. She said, "It's a meal ready to eat, ain't you ever seen one?"

"Whut?"

"There's food in there," she said.

I sighed and said, "You figure it out on your own. We're busy and we got friends coming, so git back to your clearing and don't come back here. You think I don't got ammo in here?"

"I'm going," he said, more intrigued by the MRE than my gun.

Long ago, we would have been burying that man by then.

When he was well out of earshot, I turned to the handyman and said, "You know he saw your bunker, right?"

"Whut?" she asked.

"He saw the entrance to your secret stash," I said. "Why'd you throw him that MRE?"

"He said he was hungry," she said.

"He knows exactly what's going on here," I assured her. "He saw us coming out of that bunker and cover it up, and you gave him an MRE. He'll be back, and he's gonna have plenty of time to get into that bunker."

The handyman looked concerned for a short while as she processed what I said, but I could sense her disbelief. People tended to not believe things they didn't like to think about, or that they felt was beyond their control. So she formed disbelief in her mind, and then said, "You don't know that. I didn't see him when we came out of there."

I knew it was pointless to try to convince her, so I didn't. "Ok."

That, of course, convinced her a little. "Well what do we do?"

"Nothing to do," I said. "Kill him. But I'm not doing it. Hope he can't break in."

She looked fairly well crestfallen but I couldn't do anything to help her. She'd been found out, and there's not much you can do after that. That was the danger of hoarding stuff. You get that itch to sit on it, dragon-like, always chained to it so you can protect it from other people who you don't want to have it. You build up a safe-house around it, you lock yourself inside. Pretty soon you end up like that crazy mountain-man, unwashed and toothless, delusional and piteous. But damn it, you have your stuff and nobody else can get to it.

And that's pretty much all you've got.

Chapter 14. KCG

We were soon back on the road, backtracking as I'd anticipated, in order to get back to the main road. We kept a watchful eye out for the mountain-man, just in case he wasn't as innocent as he'd seemed and actually intended to attempt some kind of ambush. Sometimes the random strays you meet like that mountain-man were more frightening than a crank. At least the cranks banded together and acted in a fairly predictable manner; not any less threatening, really, but at least they had sensible, if not misguided, goals. Strays, on the other hand, could do anything, without any reason whatsoever. You never knew exactly what was going on inside their heads.

Once we'd reached the main road and were well on our way along that, I mused about the mountain-man. He was obviously a stray, so he pre-dated the Revolution. He'd probably just been finishing up his training and ready to enter the "real world" when suddenly there was no "real world" any more. It was swept right out from underneath him. Maybe he'd fought on one side or another, or maybe he'd just run, and ended up in those very woods, and has been there ever since.

I wondered what he might have intended for his life. Not being a stray, that much was certain. I didn't know what historically people's desires were. Classically, at least from what the Children of Elektronix had taught me, it was a vehicle, a house all to themselves, a woman or two, and as much stuff as they could hoard. Anyone who didn't want these things, was considered, by and large, crazy. Or worse yet, a revolutionary.

The handyman was quiet as we walked, probably thinking of her stash up in the mountain. She wouldn't be able to get over that fever for a few days, at least, I anticipated.

We walked for a while, until we came upon a little vending stand along the side of the road. They were real people, and seemed to be giving away fruit. There were two of them; an old man and, presumably, his daughter.

"Fruit?" the old man called to as we approached.

After we made a careful surveyance of the stand and the two people behind it, we approached. The handyman fondled some of the fruit to see if it was good. I said, "Why are you giving away fruit?"

"We had too much, didn't want it to go to waste," the old man said.

I waited for the rest of the story.

His daughter spoke up: "We'd appreciate donations if ya'll got anything, like, clean water, med supplies, anything useful really."

The handyman was smelling a pear, seemed to approve. She turned her back to them to dig into her backpack, took out a box of band-aids, turned back. "Ya'll need these?"

The old man took the box and opened it, looked at the contents. "We could use these, I guess."

"I'll take two pears then?"

"OK," the old man said. "Thanks."

The handyman picked out two good pears and gave me one. I thanked her.

"Close to KCG, are we?" I asked the vendors.

"Bout three miles down that way," the daughter said. "Why? you goin' there?"

"Not really, just figured there had to be some town near if ya'll are out here on the road like this. Why not give the fruit away in town?"

"Walk three miles with fruit to give away?" the girl asked. "Nah, easier to give it out here. We live just that way." She point behind them off to the horizon.

I looked down the road in the direction of KCG. "Three miles, you say?"

"Maybe more like four or five," the old man said.

"Then I guess we better keep walking," I said. "I'd like t'make it in time for the evening broadcast."

"If you hurry, you can make it," the girl said. "I bet. Ya'll want a orange fer free?"

The handyman and I thanked them for the pears and the orange, and we resumed our journey.

Four or five miles out of town could mean that they had no idea whether or not the broadcasts were happening or not, but it somehow struck me as odd that they wouldn't know the broadcasts were happening.

"You got that radio handy?" I asked the handyman as we walked.

"Sure."

"How 'bout giving a listen to KCG?" I said. "See if they're broadcasting anything."

"What would they be broadcasting this time of day?" she asked as she dug out her radio.

"I don't know, a call for a new commie?"

She wound up the radio as we walked, and then tuned into KCG's frequency. Dead air.

"When was the last time we checked?" I asked.

"Last night, I reckon," she said. "Nothing then."

"We were behind that mountain, up in the woods though," I said, thinking aloud. "You think that mighta interfered if there was a broadcast?"

"Yeah probably," she said. "I don't know."

"You think they got a powerful station?" I asked, knowing the answer. I could have spouted off the specs of KCG in my sleep.

She pointed ahead. "Watch."

After the next few hill crests, I started to see rising above the horizon great, powerful wings, swirling slowly in the breeze. Heavy and labored, these giant metal beasts churned, the windmills of KCG. At first there was but one, and then another. And then, like an explosion, when we reached the next hill, there were fields of them. It was dizzying and blinding in the sunlight, and we could literally hear them at work.

The windmills were white, and they glistened in the sun. And they guided us along the road like the pillars of an ancient temple. And soon, even from this distance, we could see the tall, proud radio tower rising over the horizon, standing alone as it had for so long, its intricate crossbeams silhouetted against the sky. We were near KCG now, and soon, we would know why the transmissions had ceased.

Chapter 15. Inn9

> Aiming at implacable revolution, the revolutionary may and frequently must live within society, pretending to be completely complacent to it, for the revolutionary must penetrate everywhere, into all the higher and middle-classes, into the houses of commerce, the churches, and the palaces of the aristocracy, and into the worlds of the bureaucracy and literature and the military, and also into the Third Division and the Winter Palace of the Czar.
>
> — The Revolutionary's Catechism

We arrived in KCG proper as the evening fell. The streets were mostly empty, then, but we kept an eye out for doors with the Inn mark on them. We stopped at the first well-populated one we saw, wanting, as we did, some company to help us learn about KCG.

I could tell she was excited to be in KCG, and I had to remind myself that to her, this was a big city. This was the metropolis, with machines and mechanics and a well-known radio tower. This was a place she had aspired to reach, and now she was here, along with the confidence that came along with the companionship of a streetsmart friend like...well, me.

So I diplomatically suggested to the handyman that we didn't mention too much about why we were there just yet. She couldn't understand why not, but I convinced her that sometimes listening was more informative than talking, and sometimes asking questions led people to say things that might not necessarily be true. So we'd just go in and listen for a while, see what people were talking about, and then maybe start asking some questions.

She eventually seemed to concede to what I was requesting, so we went into inn9, waded through the small crowd of people sitting at their cafe tables drinking and talking and playing chess and reading and doing all the things people did in the evening. There was a three-person band off in the corner, playing a variety of stringed instruments and generally giving the cafe an atmosphere that made you want to stay there for the evening, to relax, and be with friends.

We approached the bar. The old woman looked up from her book. "Yes?"

"You got room for two overnight guests?" I asked.

"Well, there are some beds in the room upstairs, on the right. You go on in there and see if a bunk is available. If so, you put yer stuff on it so as t'claim it, and then ya'll comes back down and we'll see if we got'ny food for ya."

"We just ate," I said. "What about to drink? What've you got?"

"Well I'm out of coffee," she admitted. "I been out all week long. But I got the regular hot chocolate I kin make, and juice, and things like that. Warm milk, too. Pretty fresh."

"You got coffee?" I asked the handyman. I thought I'd seen coffee in her bunker.

The handyman considered the question and I knew she had a brick of ground beans in her bag but was considering whether the beds and a hot drink was worth a brick of coffee. She shrugged a little and said, "I got a brick of it from that merchant on the road, just outside town."

The woman's eyes brightened.

The handyman carefully opened her bag and phished around in it, and eventually brought forth the vacuum-sealed brick of coffee she'd taken from her bunker. She looked at it as if to make sure it was in good enough condition to give away, and then put it on the counter in front of the woman.

The woman was clearly pleased, and grateful. "If there ain't a bunk upstairs ya'll let me know, I got some cots in the back."

We thanked her and went upstairs. The first room was the public sleeping space, and it looked like there were a few fairly permanent residents there. But there were a few bunks that looked unused. So we claimed them with our backpacks.

"If you're hungry, we should eat up here," I said. "I think the coffee was a smart trade, I don't want to have to give away too much food."

"I'll split another MRE with you," she suggested.

We opened an MRE and wolfed it down cold. I let her have the soup packet because it had meat in it and I was feeling a little sick of meat again. I ate most everything else, but we split the fruitcake packet. After that, both of us were ready for a drink, so we went back downstairs and could smell the coffee brewing.

Fortunately, the old woman had made a full pot of coffee. Most people there got pretty excited about it, so the handyman and I felt pretty good about the trade. That was the thing about not hoarding stuff. If you give it away when it's really needed, then you usually get paid back with more gratitude that you know what to do with. No brick of ground coffee has ever made me feel good about myself, but giving a brick of coffee away and sharing it with an entire cafe in need of coffee, that earned us some friends, so case in point.

The old woman gave us credit for the gift, so everyone warmed up to us immediately. We heard a few dozen variations of the story about why they had no coffee and how they'd expected to get some from a coffee distributor that sometimes passed through, but he hadn't come by last week and so they'd been without coffee for a good two or three weeks, depending on who you asked.

As for who the guests were, some of them had become locals who had no place to stay and so they stayed there. They were mostly artists and theorists, and not just a few of them had some kind of physical limitation to actually taking shifts in a work crew. A very long time ago, they'd have been those people who just fell through the cracks of that old, "modern" society. They might have been supported, more or less, by their owners but mostly they'd have just scraped by. Others would have lived short lives. But now they have everything they need, same as everyone else. And what they can contribute, they do.

One of the artists had painted the Inn markers on every inn-house in the city. They'd been elaborate markers, using the standard Xorg iconography but done with a unique style and character for each building.

And the band in the corner played every day and every night either out on the street or in a cafe. There was music, they said, in the city all day long, on every street corner. It must have sounded magical during the day.

One of the men in a wheelchair said he was learning to write, so as to do stock accounting for the cafe. He felt they needed a better system to track what they used and how often and when people came through the city and so on. It was his project, and he was going to make it happen, even if it took having to learn to write and do math.

Everyone there had their own story to tell. Their own reason for being in KCG, in that inn, that night. And if you asked anyone how they were, they said, "Can't complain."

That was the standard response these days. "Can't complain." It meant that you had what you needed in life; you had food, shelter, friends, and purpose.

Purpose was important. That had been something the Revolutionaries had had to teach people: to find their purpose. For a while they said "Find your Art" because the Revolutionaries who were making up the signs and things were themselves artists and didn't know that most people didn't think about art. Most people didn't think of what they did as art. Even though it was true; everyone does art, everyone is an artist in their own way. The man learning to write to do stock tracking, that was an art. He was an artist. But he wouldn't have said so, couldn't accept the idea that something like that could be considered an art form rather than a simple act of contribution to the inn that he called home.

So they'd changed it to "Find your Purpose" because everyone liked the idea that they might have an actual, useful purpose. And the idea, back then -- or the implication -- was that as long as you found your purpose, then you'd have everything you needed in the world. Because you were contributing to your fellow human, so they would contribute back to you. And you know, it was true.

Later there arose, of course, the people who decided it was their purpose to have no purpose. And no one could argue with them, because if that was what they said their purpose was, then that was that. Sometimes it seemed that their real purpose was to be annoying, and so some of these people weren't welcome in some places, and that started happening often enough that they started revising their purpose, such that they started doing little chores here and there just to make amends.

Things like that have a way of smoothing themselves out.

Chapter 16. Radio Silence

I asked the group of Inn guests where the radio was, but no one seemed to know of one. I asked the old woman, and she said she had one but that she'd have to find it.

I was more than a little surprised at the apathy. Before I'd gone up to my mountaintop, the daily broadcasts had been big events. Everyone tuned into the daily broadcasts to find out what was happening with other towns, who needed what kind of supplies, whether or not there were dangerous elements on the move, and so on.

That no one even could find a radio disappointed me a little. I had no illusion that people in KCG should actually care about what the weather in KPX or KDE or any other far city, I had no illusion that by listening to the broadcasts the world was united under a common banner. Quite the contrary, that kind of false media overlay was one thing the commies and the Children of Elektronix both had fought against. But, at least as commies, we had the secret impression that we were reaching everyone on the planet. To find an entire inn of guests who hadn't heard a daily broadcast in months suggested that there might be more people out there who didn't listen. And that meant there were people well out of the reach of commies.

Out of reach of commies. This could be a good thing, but it sounded bad to me. How would people take care of one another without some kind of information about what was going on around them?

Looking around me, however, I couldn't see a problem. People were being taken care of, there was comradeship, the people had banded together locally. That was what the Children of Elektronix had fought for. That was what we'd wanted, and sought to create when we destroyed the institutions that had bound together the sense of nationalism and widespread unity. We splintered the world, we divided it into millions of little towns, each independent and mostly self-sufficient. No need for nationalism, no need for government. No need for anything more than shelter, food, friendship, and purpose.

The theory was that radio signals only go so far, really. They actually go quite far depending on atmospheric conditions and the strength of the originating signal, but in terms of conveniently getting a strong signal, it only really only lasts for a certain distance. And then it fades, and because it has no real effect on your local community after a certain distance, there's really no reason for you to hear it anyway.

But then again, wasn't there a need for some kind of unifying message? Gentle reminders about a person's responsibility to the world that they live in? Or would that be carried on regardless of a broadcast. Or would it die in spite of a broadcast.

The old woman emerged from a back room with a small handset radio. I wound it up for a while, and then tuned into the local frequency. Usually it would have music to my ears, but this time it utterly shocked and confounded me: the broadcast was playing over the air just as usual, as if nothing had ever been wrong at all.

The handyman and I sat at the table, hunched over the little handset, listening carefully. It was a current broadcast, there was no doubt about it. There was no mention of previous radio silence.

"Go up to your radio and see if you're getting this," I told the handyman.

She went upstairs and was gone for a while, came back. "It's real. I'm gettin' it too."

I turned to a man sitting nearby and sipping his coffee. He looked back at me curiously. I said, "Was there an outage of the broadcasts recently? For, maybe, a few days?"

"Don't know. I don't listen to 'em."

"Well," I said, "do you know who the commie is?"

"Not exactly. I think his name's Rick."

That would have been rkicr on the commie list. Of course I'd talked to him before, and I knew his name and call-sign well. But if he'd passed on into the great Dev Null one way or another, or just walked away from the job, or had been injured, I wanted to know about it.

"We couldn't pick up a signal on the way in," the handyman said. "Maybe we oughta file a bug with Rick, huh?"

The man shrugged. "Might as well. If somethin's broken on his rig he oughta know about it."

"Well it'd be nice if we knew where to find him, maybe had an introduction," she said.

"I don't know him," the man said. He looked around, saw someone who might be able to help, and called him over. The second man, older and in a wheelchair with the name "Dave" stenciled on the back, rolled up casually.

"You the ones who brought the coffee?" Dave asked.

"Yep," the handyman said.

Dave glanced at her and I could see his primary interest shifting away from coffee. He said, "Well then what can I do for you?"

Dave was a veteran, I figured. He'd obviously figured out how to survive a good long time after the war and whatever injury crippled him. He was strong and handsome, and confident. I admired these qualities in anybody, but he was too busy admiring the handyman to take much notice of me.

"We need to talk to the commie," I said, breaking in because I knew the handyman would've mentioned too much of something. Either she'd have given him the full story on why we were there, or tipped him off as to who we *thought* the commie was, or some detail that nobody really had the business of knowing one question into a relationship.

Dave looked at me, then back at the handyman, then at us both. "What do you wanna talk to Rick for?"

I wondered, if Rick was the commie still, why he wasn't broadcasting at full power and why he hadn't sent word of a change in his station's output. I wondered if this was going to be the same Rick I thought I knew via radio, and how I'd even know one way or another.

The handyman gave Dave the reason for needing to see Rick, and asked if could introduce us to Rick the next day.

"I'll take you over to the station," Dave said. "He doesn't generally like company but I think he might make an exception for you."

Of course Rick didn't like company. He was a commie.

"Where'll we find you tomorrow?" the handyman asked.

"I was kinda hoping you'd just kinda wake up with me." And that was Dave. Straight out of the old world, trying to apply the lessons he'd been taught as a military man to the modern day.

"What d'you mean?" the handyman asked. She wasn't trying to be funny or elusive. She actually did not understand. She had no basis for the awkward social advances of an old world man.

Dave considered this for a moment, and then he said, "Well I figured we could all sleep in the same room, there's at least one extra bunk in the downstairs room where I stay."

"Well we'd need two anyway," the handyman said. "'Sides we already claimed two bunks upstairs. You'll be at breakfast?"

"Yeah, I'll be here," he said. "Early. What do you want for breakfast? I'll have Ma Bell make you up some."

"What ever," the handyman said. "We'll eat anything."

"OK, I'll tell her to make enough for you. Why not come on over to my table and have a drink?"

The handyman shrugged and followed Dave back to his table. I had no intention of becoming the handyman's butch, so I stayed at my table and talked to some of the other guests.

Eventually people started turning in for the night, and when that happens in an inn it usually behooves everyone to follow suit, simply so you don't trip over each other trying to find your bunk. I stood and waved at the handyman as a farewell, but she took it as a chance to extricate herself away from Dave. She and I went upstairs.

There were a few people in their bunks already, two of them already snoring, and another looked half-asleep. I laid down on my bunk, and the handyman laid on hers in such a way that our heads were close. She bridged the gap until her head was on my bunk, next to my own.

"Dave's a war veteran," she said in a low voice so as not to disturb the other bunkers.

"I figured. You know he was making a sexual comment when he said he wanted you to wake up next to him?"

"Is that what he meant?" she asked. "Wonder why he didn't just say so."

"Cuz that's not how it used to work," I said.

"How did it used to work?"

"It didn't."

She said, "Well, he fought on the Army side. Against the militia."

"If he did that, how come he's still around?" I asked. "Not like his side won."

"He'll tell you all about it if you ask him, I guarantee."

"Well maybe I will, tomorrow at breakfast," I said. "But right now I guess we should get some sleep."

We both closed our eyes and I could feel myself drifting off into sleep. The handyman's voice brought me back a little to consciousness: "You think Rick might need some help?"

"Who?"

"Rick, the commie. Think he might need some help around the station?"

"I don't know," I said. "Probably not."

I said that so I wouldn't build up her hopes needlessly. I figured she had a lot to learn and Rick probably wasn't the type to teach a noob. Besides, I was starting to think I might need an apprentice myself, and there was no point in pawning a good one off.

Chapter 17. Breakfast with Dave"

> By a revolution, the Society does not mean
> an orderly revolt according to the classic
> western model – a revolt which always stops
> short of attacking the rights of property and
> the traditional social systems of so-called
> civilization and morality. Until now, such a
> revolution has always limited itself to the
> overthrow of one political form in order to
> replace it by another, thereby attempting to
> bring about a so-called revolutionary state. The
> only form of revolution beneficial to the people
> is one which destroys the entire State to the
> roots and exterminated all the state traditions,
> institutions, and classes.
>
> — The Revolutionary's Catechism

The next morning, the handyman and I arose at more or less
the same time, and gathered our things. We went downstairs
and arrived while the host was still making breakfast. Ma Bell
was what they called the host; this turned out to be a play on
"Mabel", her real name, but since she was a sort of a mother-
figure of the Inn, most of the regulars had modified her name
to be Ma Bell instead. I'd learned that bit of trivia the previous
night from some of the people I'd talked to over coffee. You can
learn all kinds of things when people are eating and drinking
together.

I often wondered how many wars in the old world could have
been avoided if the owners of the people, who I guess they
used to call Prime Ministers or Chairmen or Presidents, would
have just sat down together and had a really good meal. And
by "good" I don't mean over-elaborate. I just mean good. Good
food, well prepared, by Ma Bell or someone like her.

Ma Bell turned out to be an expert cook, and you could tell
she loved it more than anything. She made us oats, and toast
with honey, with some pears on the side. It looked, smelled, and

tasted like it would have distracted people from making war, that's for sure.

As we ate, I talked war with Dave. His breed was fading, and soon there would be no more real stories from people who'd actually lived in the old world. So I asked him about his experiences in the war, and told him that the handyman had told me he'd fought for the wrong side.

"Yeah, I was in the army alright. They called it the U.S. Army, at the time. Now eventually that got split, itself, into two different entities, but I stayed on with the U.S. Army, although I had not just a few friends who switched over to Canada-Corp and tried to help out the North."

I was vaguely familiar with this, but he must have seen my blank expression, because he moved on in his story quickly: "I was up against the People's Militia, and somebody got me, right through the back, with a pretty sizable bullet. Tore lots of stuff -- skin, muscle, a vertebra. Turns out that vertebra it got, that was the one that makes legs work. So mine don't. Anyway, I got sent to a hospital in the city and I was there for about a week, I think."

"What hospital?"

"They called the city itself Pittsburgh. Or I think it was Pittsburgh. It might have been another city, but it was in that area anyway. Anyway, back in those days you didn't have radios, you had television."

"What's a television?" the handyman asked.

"It's like a panel, flat, but...it had pictures on it. It's like a radio only with pictures."

"Pictures of what? weather conditions?"

"Well, sometimes, yes, they'd have pictures of the weather. Other times it was just a person, talking."

"A commie?"

"No, a...a person. Just any person."

"I don't understand," the handyman said.

"Well somebody had to read the information," Dave said. "So they'd just get somebody to read it out loud, and they'd show the person's picture while they read."

"That don't make a whole lotta sense," the handyman said. "But go on."

"I didn't say it made sense," Dave said and smiled. "Well, I was in the hospital, and all the television -- the broadcasts -- I'd seen up until that point, they were positive, you know? They made you feel good about the war, they told you that the militia was being defeated on all fronts. But the day I was awake enough to listen to the reports in the hospital, they were actually admitting that the militia might be doing alright. That the U.S. Army wasn't winning. That it was a tough fight.

"And then 'bout the middle of that week, it went from bad to worse, just all of a sudden. I mean, one minute the U.S. Army was carefully studying the situation to see how they could bring this complex fight to a swift close, and the next minute, they were talking about people evacuating cities. Mass exoduses out of entire regions. Suddenly all the footage -- the pictures, you know? -- all the pictures were of people getting the hell out. They were all moving. Where? I don't know. Anyway, it turned out most of them were really either in the militia or sympathizers of the militia anyway, so they weren't really running from anyone but whatever Army laid claim over them.

"And that's when I realized that I'd been claimed by an army, too. In my case, it was the U.S. Army, but it could have been any army. And I realized then and there that I'd been on the wrong side, and that if I was gonna belong to any side, it was gonna be the people's side. The people's army.

"The 'militia' they called it.

"Round the same time, the hospital decided it needed to evacuate. Imagine that? a whole hospital, evacuating? They took a lot of the patients with them. Some others stayed. Some others, I think they just pulled the plug on 'em. But me, I hid, so I could stay. And once the officials of that hospital were gone, I found out which wing was the militia POW wing -- that's 'Prisoners Of War' -- and I waltzed right in there and joined up that very day."

He finished his story with an air of pride. He considered himself a hero for switching sides to the winning army just before the war ended. He maintained his overly-significant pause for a few moments, and then resumed eating his breakfast.

"Sounds like any body would've," I said.

"Would've what?" he asked, so surprised that oatmeal dribbled a little from his mouth.

The handyman got up, ostensibly for more coffee, but as soon as she was out of his view, emphatically shook her head at me. She knew where I was going, and I guess she'd started to know what to expect from me. I ignored her gracefully.

"Well, you switched sides to the winning one, right as the city was being evacuated. Who wouldn't do that?"

I imagine he'd thought about that very question for a long time by then. He said: "In the old world, a lot of men wouldn't have done it. Because in the old world, they'd told us how we owed the Army everything. And we didn't argue, because as far as we knew, they were right. But seeing the people run from the Army instead of from the militia? that changed it for me. That's when I realized the militia was the people, and the people were what we were supposed to be fighting for. I've been militia ever since, I guarantee you that."

"Why were the people running from the Army?" the handyman asked.

"Because the army didn't know who was militia and who wasn't, so they just shot everybody," Dave said. "See the militia didn't have uniforms, they didn't have ranks, or tanks, sometimes they didn't even have guns. And somebody could become militia at a moment's notice." He snapped his fingers. "One moment I'm sitting here having coffee with you. Next minute, I'm gouging out your eyes with this coffee spoon. That's how it was happening. I don't know if it was by design, if this militia, whoever they were, had planted that many people in the general public -- sleepers we used to call 'em, where they'd look and act like normal people until they were ordered somehow to actually act and be militia. Or maybe it was just catching on, this idea that the people had formed a secret, invisible militia, and it was completely open source, and all you had to do to become part of the militia was to do militia-like things when appropriate."

"When did the militia draft the GPL?" I asked. I knew the answer to a very specific date and the name of the man who'd signed it, but nobody but a commie would know these things.

Dave shrugged. "I don't know how that came about. I think it pre-dates the Revolution. It was a commie thing. They'd drafted it...or really their precursors, 'hackers' they called them. It didn't get adopted by the People until after the Revolution, when people realized they needed some kind of code to live by, so they adopted that because it was what the commies were using and it seemed to work for them."

"Speaking of commies," I said. "Should we be go finding ours?"

Like the old world man he was, Dave said firmly, "Let's do it."

Chapter 18. Rkicr

The walk through early morning KCG was leisurely, partly because we were going at Dave's relaxed pace, and partly because there was much to see. The handyman hadn't seen a real city before, and I hadn't seen one in a very long time.

Stories of what cities used to be like were common, but rarely filled with any nostalgia. They were not, as far as I knew, hyperbolic, either. Apparently there was no need to be. People really did live on the streets because they'd been unable to meet the extortionist demands of a "landlord". Of course, in the old world, people were thought to own land, and you weren't allowed to be on that land unless you paid charter. The government and its agents being, of course, the perpetual exception to this rule.

The city that had formed here within KCG was like many of the other modern cities. They'd kept the best of the old, improved it, mostly, and constructed new ways of interpreting buildings and city design.

Used to be that cities sprung up as a reaction to increase in population and economics. This typically made for badly designed cities that were both difficult to navigate and oppressive to the psyche. Imagine the poor of the city being relegated to ghettos, and having to travel an hour into the city on crammed trains every day just to serve their masters. Imagine these poor having to plan an entire day just to make their way from their ghettos to get to the shopping centers of a city, which have been placed for the convenience of only the rich. Imagine the rich of the city residing in penthouses on the 80th floor of tall buildings, living high above the misery of the city below, while the poor labourers swarmed in the streets desperate for food and clothing.

There was an obscenity to that kind of psychological implication of a city, but there was also a technical aspect to this as well; things that commies tended to belabor in their spare time. Cities designed as a reaction to economics and population tended to be very inefficient. There were power stations and water cleaning plants and trains and streets placed haphazardly to accommodate the growth, regardless of what they meant for the overall workflow of the city. People swarmed around in the city, trying to get to where they needed to go in spite of where they were forced to live for caste and economic reasons. Bottlenecks occurred in every kind of traffic, so the roads or pipelines or services were expanded hastily again. But of course the answer was never to just open up the bottleneck, because in so doing you simply invite more traffic and encounter another bottleneck.

The answer was well thought-out city design. And that's what most cities are working on now. Perfection of layout, perfection in city planning, design, urban engineering, building design, interiour design. It is an evolving process, still considered to be in beta, but it is something. There is effort being made, which is a lot more than you could say for the old world.

That's what the handyman was seeing as we walked through the city; the new world's answer to city planning. I felt proud, for some reason. Not that I'd really ever thought that much about it aside from what the Children of Elektronix had instilled in me, and certainly I'd never had any part in city planning. But I felt ownership of it anyway.

Because in the new world, everything belonged to everyone, and private property was theft.

When we arrived at the radio station of KCG, Dave used the intercom to introduce himself and notify Rkicr that he had two guests with him. We waited outside the door for a while and began to believe we might not be let in, but the door eventually was unlatched and unlocked and unfettered and finally swung open.

Rkicr was every bit a commie as I'd imagined. He was pale, balding, bearded, and probably hadn't showered in days. I knew that general state well enough. While I tried to maintain some personal dignity, I will admit that when you have no visitors, hygiene starts to matter less than important things like checking data streams, scanning transmissions, twisting cable, sending insipid messages to other commies, reading ebooks and manuals, and all the other things you can fill time with so effortlessly.

"What can I do for you?" he asked, not politely.

"These two visitors to our city wanted to speak to the commie in charge."

"Well that would be me," Rkicr conceded.

"Did you know your signal wasn't being received anywhere beyond the windmills or thereabouts?" I said.

"Did you check your radio," he said with finality.

"Did you check yours?" I asked just as firmly.

"You know, we do a little more than just press the 'broadcast' button, we comm techies," he said. "I know that's hard to believe."

"What exactly do you do?" I asked, trying to sound rude. It was a cheap trick but his particular brand of commie pride gave me the idea that if I doubted his technical capability loudly enough, he'd invite us in to witness his greatness.

"I run maintenance checks on all software and hardware," he said, more calmly. I could tell he'd checked his ego, which was good for the general reputation of commies, but bad for my immediate goals. "Every day."

"Could I see inside your lab?" the handyman said. "I been wantin' to see inside a radio station forever."

"Why would you want to see a bunch of boring wires and control panels?" he asked.

"I'm a handyman," she said, "hoping to transition into becoming a commie."

Rkicr looked over at Dave. Dave gave him a reassuring look. Rkicr backed into his station a little, saying, "I don't have all day, I'm pretty busy, I have some diagnostics to run and I bent a BNC earlier today so i have to fix that before evening. You can come in for a little while though."

We all followed him inside, closing and securing the door behind us. His control room was up a set of stairs, and he apologized to Dave that there was no easy way up but that he could pull Dave's chair up if he wanted. Dave declined, saying that he'd seen radio gear before.

So the handyman and Rkicr and I went upstairs to master controls, the place where Rkicr ran the entire comm station and also had access to most of the vital bare metal and wires. It was a mess, of course, with spare parts lying on any otherwise empty surface, half-disassembled audio monitors and compressors and receivers and tuners, cables everywhere. Rkicr was a pack-rat, that much was obvious. It didn't look like he'd ever traded anything in. It looked, instead, like he'd kept every item of anything he'd ever come into contact with, and simply used whatever he had to fix whatever broke. He was the type of commie who, if he had a blown-out board, he'd just have just melted down some random piece of metal, formed his own strip, and repaired the board. I admired those commies on one hand, but also generally regarded them as bat-shit crazy at the same time since it was generally easier to just strip another board for parts.

"Don't touch anything," Rkicr warned us as we entered. He started giving us a brief tour of the control room. He pointed to a rack housing a host of different monitoring boxes and said, "Eina's is my monitoring rack. She's got all the info about amplitude, wattage, levels, frequency, modulation, and so on. Evas' the rack with my processors; I can adjust noise gate, pipe it through a compressor, leveler, and whatever LADSPA or LV2 chain I've got up and running on any given day. Ecore is my power backup unit. Embryo is the receiving rack, it's got all my tuners, backup tuners, and the brain of my konsole."

He looked at us both. "Now do either of you actually know enough about this gear to double-check my work? or are you going to just have to take my word for it?"

The handyman shrugged, "I think it all looks great. I wish I did understand it all."

In the meantime, I was scanning the rack he called Eina; his monitoring boxen. It all looked good, it all read normal. He was right about that. He was definitely sending the signal he believed he was sending, unless his monitoring gear was severely misaligned.

"How do you zero out a monitor?" I asked.

"What do you mean 'zero out'?" he asked, although I knew he was well aware of what I meant. I could see in his face a hint of surprise that I'd asked the question, but he was playing the usual commie game of asking more questions than providing answers. As always, I could and did respect that.

"How do you know your monitors aren't reading one hundred percent only because they still read 50% when nothing's happening, instead of zero?"

"Oh, you mean how do I determine the baseline," he said, using an alternate term for the same thing so it sounded like I had used the wrong term.

"Sure, I guess," I said. "Indulge me; I'd just like to see a negative before I see a positive."

He walked over to the output monitor and flipped the input to a non existent channel. The VU meter's needle fell all the way to the zero marker. He flipped it back to its usual input and the needle rose back up to where it had been.

"That's how you confirm that zero is in fact zero," he said. "Any more questions?"

The handyman, still vying for a job, chimed in: "Not that I can think of. I think it's a great setup. Wish I had a place like this."

If the monitors were correct, then he was definitely sending out a signal, and yet I was definitely not receiving it, and he was not receiving signal back from me to tell him about it, then the only answer was that somehow we were not able to communicate with one another. There just wasn't much that could cause that sort of breakage, and I wasn't really sure what it could be. Aside from a mountain or sheer distance, and neither of those two things seemed very likely.

"You've got no pingback device," I said.

"A what?" he said. I could almost sense him starting to theorize that I was a commie or a commie-in-training.

"You know, something out there in the field to tell you that it's receiving the signal. Something to provide positive feedback on your transmission's success."

He sat down at his konsole and typed in a few commands. The black screen filled with green text, changing every moment as different signals got read in and dumped onto the screen. He motioned at it, and then said, "This is why non-commies don't run radio stations. Don't you know that I've got about a hundred 'pingback' devices out in the field? they're called 'other radio towers'."

He stood and walked over to an old map on the wall with little pins and marks all over it. "Every single one of these radio towers, and each repeater, and each comm station, is, basically, a pingback device. If one tower doesn't get my broadcast, I hear about it. Not just from that tower's operator, but a few operators, because commies actually communicate. Yes, communication technicians actually communicate on a regular basis. You name one tower. Any tower, now, you take your pick. And I'll tell you who operates it. Go ahead."

"KMT," I said.

"KMT.....that's a repeater station," he said, thinking aloud. "Run by...ender, or Enid. Ender's her callsign."

That was me. Ender, or, as he said, Enid, by birth.

"Well what if this Ender wasn't receiving your signal," I said, "and he tried to send you a message that he wasn't getting it, but you didn't get that message?"

"Then some other tower would let me know that they were getting a signal from me," he said. "And, Ender's not a he, Ender's a she."

"How do you know?"

"Because she refers to her gear by men's names. Male commies tend to refer to their boxen as females."

I sheepishly made a mental note of that. Not that it mattered, but it was a matter of pride for a commie to reveal no information about herself without being aware of it. It was hard not to form relationships with your radio equipment, though, and I always preferred to anthropomorphize them as males rather than females; I always thought of them as hard-working men, toiling away like those classic male figures did, sweating but cheerful, full of strength and stamina. It was romanticism upon romanticism. And it had given away at least one detail about Ender. Oh well, live and learn.

"What if you weren't receiving anyone's messages about it?" I persisted.

He simply blinked.

"How would that even be possible?" the handyman asked. "I mean, step outside, turn on a radio. It ain't that hard, you'd get a message."

"I talk to these people every day," Rkicr said. He got up and started shuffling us toward the stairs. "And speaking of that, I do have a comm station to manage here."

"I'll bet you haven't talked to Ender in about 12 days," I said.

Rkicr stopped dead in his tracks. He said, "You stay right there."

He walked back to his konsole, grepped through some log files, and then came back over to me. "So why would you say I haven't talked to Ender in 12 days?"

"I'm from KBV area," I said. "I was helping out the commie there, and we haven't heard from Ender either, not for about 12 days."

"Then why don't you go check on KMT? Maybe Ender put her finger in an electrical socket and got fried. I don't really see what I can do to help you out in KBV."

"Well, we're not receiving your signal either," I said.

"And we couldn't pick it up on the road out here, either," the handyman said.

Rkicr considered what we'd said now. Absently, he said, "Lemme see your radio."

The handyman dug her radio out from her backpack and handed it to him. He started winding it, still deep in thought. When it had enough juice, he tuned it, almost without having to look at it, to KCG. He walked over to his konsole, typed in a command, and the radio blurted out a KCG identification.

"OK so your radio works," he said. "And my radio works. So either you two are nutty, or there's something very strange going on."

He gave the handyman her radio back and sat down. He motioned for us to also take seats. We did.

Chapter 19. Comm Talk

Rkicr was a smart commie. He'd revealed little and had shown me what he'd gathered from Ender. He ran a major radio station, obviously was basically a handyman himself, probably far superiour in even that than the handyman sitting next to me, and that was her full time job. And he'd been in radio longer than I had been, which I respected greatly. Running a repeater tower was one thing, but being the source of broadcasts, structuring the sound for maximum sound quality and distance, sending and trafficking all kinds of data through the air...that was an art and a craft.

But at the moment Rkicr was perplexed. From his relative silence, I got the sense that he might have had a notion, but that he was holding back. That would have been the commie thing to do.

I said to the handyman, "Tell him your theory."

The handyman cleared her throat because Rkicr hadn't acknowledged that I'd spoken or that she was about to speak. He still didn't, but she spoke anyway: "I've traveled pretty much all around KCG, never been here, but I've been all over the perimeter of the area. And there's this one mountain, a little sunrise of here, and from certain angles, I'm pretty sure you can see a tower there."

Rkicr looked up at that. "A tower around here? Not that I'm aware of, there isn't."

"She was theorizing that if that tower was broadcasting a signal to overpower yours..." I said, not bothering to finish a sentence I knew he already understood.

"That would require quite a bit of power," he said. "And you'd be able to hear it...you said you were getting nothing on your radio."

"Maybe they're broadcasting static," the handyman said.

"Why?"

"I don't know," she said.

Rkicr looked over at me, watched me sit silently, calmly. I was not uncomfortable with being studied. He said, "You came from KBV? Who's the commie there...?"

"I thought you said you knew them all."

"I'd like to see if you do," he said flatly.

"Gwilson," I said. And that was my second slip-up as a commie.

He sat silently, eying me, being discreet with what he'd just learned about me.

It had been a slight slip-up, but I'd already talked enough like a commie to hint at it. Knowing Gunther Wilson's callsign was something that even a commie-in-training would probably not know, and while "gwilson" could have easily meant "G. Wilson", I could tell he was catching on pretty quickly. Anyway, it didn't matter much. We were both commies, we both might as well be aware of it. No real harm done. A little embarrassing for my reputation, but otherwise of no consequence.

"But I went up and visited Ender," I said.

"Really," he said with a little laugh. "How is Ender?"

"She seemed well. Didn't seem to like visitors, though."

"Most commies don't. How's her gear? How's Max?"

Max was what I called the main amplifier. "He's loud. She said she'd recently fixed it up, actually."

He seemed satisfied. So we now knew who and what each other were. It seemed like that would make for a more efficient conversation anyway. My reputation might have been safe; I'd actually just quite cleverly revealed to him that I was a commie without revealing the same fact to the handyman. And I'd done it right in front of her. Ender might have just gained some street credit among the commie ranks.

Rkicr said, "What'd Ender tell you about this? Was she picking up signals from anywhere else?"

"She said everything was normal except that the signal from KCG was just flat out missing. She sent a request for a re-send the morning she didn't receive a broadcast, and got no answer. And no more broadcasts for about 9 days."

Rkicr said, "If I didn't know better, I'd say it sounded like a man-in-the-middle."

"A what?" I asked.

"Well, like your friend here says, maybe there is a tower out there overpowering my signals. Preventing them from getting out. But to take it a step further, what this tower could be doing, too, is intercepting messages from the outside world back to me, and filtering them. Literally just dropping the messages that are asking for re-broadcasts." He paused to think, and then added, "In fact, come to think of it, other commies have been asking about my gear. I noticed it, always thought it was odd. This would explain it."

"I don't understand," I said. "Who's got that kind of wattage, and who would go to that amount of trouble to block communication between you and the rest of the world? It sounds like an enormous undertaking."

"It does sound a little paranoid," the handyman agreed.

"It actually is a very common attack," Rkicr said. "Well at least, it used to be, back in the old world. I don't see why it wouldn't be making a comeback."

"And why would they be doing it?" I asked.

"You're the world traveler," Rkicr said. "You tell me."

There were two reasons I could think of. The first was labeled Edje; this was his transmitting rack. All the broadcasts he sent out into the world came from it. He hadn't introduced us to that because, naturally, he was a commie and didn't particularly care to show strangers the rack housing all the gear used for the station's primary function.

The second was a rack labeled Enlightenment. It housed a tuner, receiver, amplifier, monitor, processor, transmitter, power backup unit, recorder, and archiver; it was a miniature comm station in itself. I focused my eyes on the receiver. It was tuned to the Godstream.

"Have you listened to that one lately?" I asked him.

He looked where I was looking, knew to be discreet. "Not lately. I record it all the time. It automatically gets archived."

"But you haven't listened to it?"

"Not lately."

"Not for the past two weeks?"

He finally understood what I was suggesting. "Why would someone want to block that? Anyone can tune in to it on any radio."

"Maybe they're not blocking it," I said. "Maybe they're adding to it. Or taking away from it."

He considered it for a while, then said, "Hell, you're as batty as the rest."

But I wasn't, I knew that. Someone was very interested in the Godstream. Why, I could not say. But someone knew that KCG had one of the strongest Godstream signals available, and so they'd set up camp right in Rkicr's backyard.

Chapter 20. Team Mates

Back at inn9, the handyman and I sat in a corner of the cafe, drinking water from tin mugs in silence. The handyman, I could tell, was both impressed and upset by the amount of knowledge I'd shown at the radio station. And I think she'd wanted to magically get recruited as an apprentice, so when Rkicr showed us to the door without any job offer or conclusion about the dead signal, it had been a disappointment to her.

I was quiet because I knew that something now had to be done about the interference. And it wasn't going to be enough to just overpower it in turn, or even to find out who was causing it; it had to be understood. We had to know why someone was trying to block communication in and out of KCG.

We weren't going to do it alone, though. This, I was quite certain about. If someone had cared enough to gather enough power to over-broadcast KCG, they weren't going to let a commie and a handyman walk in and shut them down.

The Children of Elektronix would have been ideal for this job. This was their specialty. Seek out the old world hold-outs, and put a stop to them. In this case, I wasn't sure what kind of hold-out this was; maybe it wasn't a hold-out at all, and just someone trying to create a new new world. Either way, the Children would have known just what to do, and how to do it quickly, cleanly, and efficiently.

But the Children were also no more. They'd disbanded long ago, before I'd retreated to my mountaintop. They'd fallen apart, and had gone out separate ways, I assume. I would have to settle for some troublemakers instead.

"Troublemakers" was a term people used to use for people who were disruptive to society, or harmful to property, or just generally destructive. It was fairly common back in the old world, because people generally didn't have what they needed to get by in life. So they had to resort to making trouble, and from that trouble tended to emerge the necessities or creature comforts of life. By necessities, I mean food, drink, clothes, and so on. Creature comforts were funny, because you just didn't often want them until someone else had them; once someone had them, then people around that person wanted to share in them, and if that person didn't share, then others tended to take. And that was what they called being a troublemaker.

In the new world, people had everything they needed. And if they did not, they could ask for what they needed and it would be provided for them. In terms of creature comforts, there weren't that many, really, but people did have some. And some people made their own. And people traded, or gave things away, or whatever they wanted to do. But generally speaking, there wasn't that much of an opportunity to be a troublemaker in the traditional sense of the word.

So the word had become re-defined. Now to be a troublemaker simply meant that you were available for dangerous tasks. That you were a thrill-seeker. Troublemakers were the people you went to when you needed a group of cranks driven out of the area, or if you needed a group of people to travel down dangerous rapids, or down into a cave, or any such activity that "normal" people just didn't care to do.

So we needed troublemakers, just a few to start out with. I got Dave working on that. He knew most everyone in the city, it seemed, and while these kinds of men-about-town I tended to distrust on one level, I did recognize that they had contacts. Whether or not they could actually vouch for any of the people they knew was a different story. It always was; people like Dave usually just recommended everyone equally, because to him there was no real difference between a friendly barmaid and a friendly troublemaker. But for my purposes, I needed a real troublemaker or two. Some people I could rely on, or at least rely on as much as I would ever rely on a complete stranger. Which is to say, not much. But I wanted numbers, and I wanted people who would go accompany me on this journey, and not get bored or scared and go home half way through.

The problem with Dave's type was that they more you impressed upon them that reliability and trustworthiness was important, the more reliable and trustworthy his adjectives became when he was describing each candidate. To buffer against this, the handyman accompanied Dave on a few of his recruiting missions, just to get a feel for where he was finding these people.

The first suitable troublemaker Dave and the handyman brought around for us was named Gidal. He was not large, but he was solid, and he knew his weapons, which encouraged me a little. The Children of Elektronix had always known their weapons, for better or for worse; either way, it was good insurance. He was a dark man in both complexion and mood, and seemed not too eager to embark on the mission with us, which I took to be a good sign. He'd clearly had a fair share of trouble such that he was no longer seeking out as much trouble as he could find, but selecting the trouble he preferred to get himself into.

I had to sell the mission to him, a little. He asked a lot of questions. I liked that.

The second suitable troublemaker Dave introduced to us was called Syck, a larger man, pleasant to talk with but obviously able to look and act imposing when required. I explained, best I could, what we were seeking to do. As for the obstacles, I wasn't sure of what those would be. The fallback term that both he and Gidal seemed to use was "backup". They were to be "backup". That sounded fine to me.

Gidal and Syck did not know each other but when the next day I invited them to have meet the handyman and me for a late breakfast, they easily fell into conversation about various daredevil events that they had in common; things like mountain climbing, base-jumping, and similar invitations to a quick death that most people in their right minds would have avoided.

By the end of the meal, they were happy with one another and seemed happy with me and the handyman as traveling partners, and so they agreed to accompany us to the location that the handyman believed was the source of the pirate signal. They required no payment or trade, except a surplus of ammunition, and food and water during the journey. The handyman discussed with them at length the different ammunition she had access to, by way of her secret stash of course, and this ultimately dictated the weaponry they agreed to bring along. I didn't say anything, but I figured if anything need blowing up, I'd be able to manage that one way or another. Blowing things up tended to be fairly easy, if you really wanted it to happen.

We agreed to leave the next morning, early.

Chapter 21. Four

The next morning, the handyman and I awakened well before dawn, gathered our things, and went downstairs into the street. It was still dark, and seeing the windmills around KCG reflecting the moonlight was enchanting. They glowed, and cast an unnatural and fluctuating silver light down around and upon the city.

We watched the windmills in the distance, until the handyman finally spoke up, "I can't figure you out quite yet."

"It usually takes people a while," I admitted.

"You're not a handyman, and you're not a commie, and you're not a troublemaker -- but you know all about doin' repairs, and all about commie equipment --"

"Gear," I said, helping her find the commie term.

"And you know all about weapons, to hear you talk to those two troublemakers we picked up. So, you been around I guess?"

I shrugged casually, "Just can't stay focused, I guess. Always poking around into different disciplines. Or maybe I just transcend classification."

She laughed. I'd noticed that whenever she thought something was absurd, she laughed.

"What did you think of Rick?" she asked. "Pretty smart, huh?"

"Knowledgeable. Maybe smart, maybe not."

"I was hopin' he might be lookin' for an assistant," she said.

"There are other commies," I said. "You just keep looking."

The white hovering glow from the windmills started to fade into the slowly lightening sky. The sun was nowhere in sight yet, but you could tell it would be rising soon. The sky was bluer than black, now, and there was a false sense of light from it.

We heard people approaching behind us, so we turned and greeted our new companions. As expected, it was Gidal and Syck, each carrying some obligatorily frightening weaponry. That was pretty much all either of them had brought. I didn't look forward to smelling either of them in three days, but at least I knew they were well armed and eager to go on the journey.

Gidal, the slighter of the two, was drinking tea from a tin mug, which he apparently kept chained to a belt loop. Syck was taking inventory of everything he had brought, looking over the things we had, taking assessment of the party.

"We ready for this?" Gidal said.

"As ready as we'll ever be," I said, invoking an old saying that people used to say to denote that they were ready to embark on their mission but really had no idea what to expect. It was a classic old saying.

"We stopping somewhere for ammo?" Syck asked.

"Yep," the handyman said. "It's out of our way but it'll be worth it for the ammo, and re-stocking on some supplies."

"Let's move," Syck said. He smiled and added to Gidal, "And hope we find some cranks along the way."

Gidal smiled, finished his tea with a gulp, grimaced at its heat, and started walking. This started us off, and we all walked in loose formation with Gidal leading and Syck taking the rear. I felt they were probably taking a simple walk out of town a little more seriously than required, but wasn't going to argue with their professionalism.

We walked in, mostly, the wrong direction, because we needed to re-stock from the handyman's stash, since we'd gained two new party members who would need food and ammo.

"A little farther sunset, we saw an encampment of cranks," I said. "They didn't look like they were on the move but..."

"Oh, we'll be ready for them if we meet them," Syck assured me.

Gidal said, "How many were there and what kind of weaponry did you see?"

"I don't know," I said. "Probably about twelve. Two vehicles. Didn't really see any weaponry, they had a scam going."

"Then they probably didn't have that much weaponry," Gidal said. "Otherwise they wouldn't have bothered trying to scam. How did you get around them?"

"Took a back road and avoided them," said the handyman. "I ain't never shot nobody and don't intend to ever have to."

"Don't you worry about that," Syck said. "That's what we're here for."

"You ever shot anyone?" Gidal asked me.

"Me? no, never," I lied. "But I've done some target practise, and I've hit it a few times."

Gidal nodded, approvingly. "That Springfield on your back ain't no toy."

"Just something I found in an abandoned house up north. Pretty powerful kick, that's for sure."

"What else you got?"

"Just a handgun," I said, and showed him my Smith and Wesson.

"That's a revolver," Gidal said, taking it and feeling it in his hand. "But it's nice. Shoot good?"

"I guess."

He gave me the gun back. "These people with the pirate tower, you think they're in for the long haul or is this just an anomaly?"

"Could be an anomaly, could the biggest crank scam ever," I said. "You never really know."

"If it's a scam, we're gonna need a lot more than the four of us," Syck said.

"I thought you said you were good?" I said jokingly.

"Oh, I'm up for it," Syck said, "If you've got the ammo, I've got the inclination."

The ammo, we had. Realistically, though, the pirate station had to have some purpose for existing. That was the thing I couldn't understand. There was no logical reason to overpower KCG, and no clear agenda in what was being broadcast on top of KCG's signal. It felt either purely antagonistic or entirely unintentional, and you don't often set up an enormous radio station unintentionally.

I feared this would not be a mission of peace.

Chapter 22. Restock

> All the gentle and enervating sentiments of kinship, love, friendship, gratitude, and even honor, must be suppressed in the revolutionary and replaced with cold and single-minded passion for revolution. For the revolutionary, there exists only one pleasure, one consolation, one reward, one satisfaction – the success of the revolution. Night and day the revolutionary must have but one thought, one aim – merciless destruction. Striving cold-bloodedly and indefatigably toward this end, the revolutionary must be prepared to destroy everything and anything that stands in the path of the revolution.
>
> — The Revolutionary's Catechism

The journey to the handyman's bunker was uneventful, with a clear road the entire way. When we arrived, I had half expected it to have been looted, but in fact it appeared to have been untouched.

We didn't reveal to the troublemakers where the bunker was, exactly, and I took them into the woods to discuss the high road, and the handyman's idea of establishing a repeater tower in this location, and other vaguely significant and important-sounding things designed solely to keep them away from the bunker site.

Of course there was no method of distraction that could allay all questions when someone returns with a backpack full of food and ammunition. I saw the look in the men's eyes when the handyman gave them their allotment of ammo, and for just a moment I felt all the muscles in my body prepare for combat or flight, or some combination thereof.

But of course the men were trustworthy and had no intention of overpowering us and claiming the handyman's bunker for themselves. They respected that we had the resources, and simply confirmed that they were satisfied with the payment.

Then we all backtracked and headed back in the general direction of KCG.

"We should avoid the main road," Syck said. "If this place is in the mountains, we should travel the mountains. Harder to keep an eye on that than a main roadway."

"Syck's right," Gidal agreed. "In the open territory, we're just a group of random travelers. On the road, we're uninvited guests."

"OK," I said, "then we'll go through the mountains. Seems like it'll be slower going that way, though."

"You in a hurry?" Gidal asked.

"No, I guess not," I said.

We stared each other down for a moment, then once Gidal decided I didn't have a secret agenda I hadn't shared, he nodded agreeably and said, "The mountains, then."

We traveled along the high road for as long as it was useful, and then veered off path into untamed territory. I decided to try my hand at garnering some free information from our new companions, not looking for anything in particular, just phishing to see what I could learn.

"I guess radio's not so important these days anyway," I said to Gidal, who was walking closest to me. "Seems like no-one I met in KCG really bothered listening to the broadcasts."

"Oh, people listen to the broadcasts," he said. "Some groups don't bother because they know the information will filter out to them eventually anyway. But most people listen to the broadcasts, mainly just to keep informed about the movement of cranks, or trade opportunities in other towns."

"You mean the people you associate with," I said. "I imagine that's a particular group; people looking for that sort of...well, trouble."

He smiled. "I don't really associate with that many troublemakers. I hate to tell you that and spoil any illusion you might have of me, but in normal, real life, I'm just a printer."

"Printer?"

"Does it surprise you that I'm literate? Yes, I print. Copies of old books, some pamphlets, things like that."

"I didn't know that was done much any more," I confessed.

He shrugged. "We do it. And we do signs for local projects, and some road signs. We also maintain traffic markers, some all-purpose painting, things like that. Basically anything that needs coloring or writing, that's what we do. We're thinking of forking the road stuff off into its own project, but until we find a project leader for that we'll wait."

The wonders of open source city engineering, or even society, never ceased to amaze me. Not because it worked so well, but that it had not always been the model. The human propensity to fill a need, to provide something that is clearly missing, is great. And the propensity for humans to join groups providing some service is great, and so the few people who begin filling a need generally grows in number in a very short time. Not every group grows naturally, of course; some must resort to near-begging and propaganda, but generally people recognize that something must get done for their own good and the greater good of their town, and they pitch in to help.

Of course, if Gidal and his associates were reviving printed matter, this meant that people were getting information from non-commie sources. Commies thought of themselves as the central communication method both locally and regionally, so to know that printed matter was making a come-back was interesting news. Something to broadcast on a commie-only channel when I got back to my mountaintop.

I wanted the handyman to chime in and ask questions, but she was playing troublemaker for the time being, her head on a swivel looking at ridges and cliffs for potential watchtowers or snipers.

"Doesn't the local radio in KCG provide advertisements and essays and other things? Why do you bother printing them?"

"Some people seem to prefer printed copies," Gidal said with a shrug. "I myself am one of them. The radio is fine, but sometimes I like to sit down at my leisure, and read something over at my own pace. Besides, I like the feel of paper."

"Paper?" I said. "That's an utter waste of materials."

"Well we're only making the paper from existing waste," he said. "We obviously aren't going to start de-forestation for it."

There was a limit, then, to how widespread the printed matter could spread. Mass production was not happening, and hopefully, for the environment's sake alone, would not happen within my lifetime, or the next generation, or the generation thereafter.

"What about you?" he asked me. "You said you came from the KBV area, helping out handymen and commies. And you came out all this way just to investigate KCG's missing signal. You must think pretty highly of the broadcasts."

"They seem to be effective," I said with a shrug. "They distribute information as far out as the information needs to be distributed. Besides, radio itself uses natural phenomena to get the information from one place to another, and it's powered by natural elements. It's the perfect medium."

"Why send information only so far?" he asked. "Why not propagate the information as far as radio can physically take it?"

"They do," I said. "Radio broadcasts from one station can be heard all over the place. We have repeater towers for that very purpose."

"But to get those broadcasts, you have to know when and where to listen. Why not aggregate selected information from various local broadcasts, and send it around on a third broadcast, a sort of all-encompassing broadcast for everyone to hear about everything going on all over the world?"

"Why would they do that? What good would it do anyone? And how would anyone possibly select information for such a worldwide broadcast? Surely that would be an impossible task in the most traditional sense of the word."

"Why?" Gidal asked.

"The minutiae is just too great," I said. "Besides, the notion is ill-conceived. Local events diminish in importance the further away from their epicenter they travel. It's a false idea that everything that occurs anywhere is significant everywhere."

"Still might be interesting to hear, from time to time," Gidal said.

"If you think that," I said, "then you are not busy enough."

We walked in a silence and I began to regret the harsh response. But it had been uttered now and was too late to take it back or to make it sound less harsh. Besides, I had meant what I'd said. The idea that hearing about events half way across the world is a romantic one; it has the initial appearance of uniting the human race. Ideally, it brings us all together, and helps us feel like progress is being made toward some imagined greater good, or it helps us be on guard against encroaching perceived enemies, or it makes us feel sad about deaths that have been said to have occurred somewhere. This is the romantic notion, the theory. The reality of it was that a commie could say anything over the radio, and once the news gets three hops distance from the source, it's beyond empirical verification anyway. It just ceases to be relevant.

There was a time in the old world when imagined threats on the other side of the world became cause for people to unite, and to manufacture weapons, and to build bunkers for themselves, and to build campaigns against this imagined threat. All without ever actually seeing the threat, without speaking with the people behind this threat.

There would even be wars over the threats. People would kill, and be killed, because they'd heard on a broadcast or read in a paper that some group of people all the way around the world were a threat to their solidarity, freedom, and system of beliefs.

I'd learnt all about propaganda. I knew its power. And I knew that very rarely was it used for the greater good.

"I leave those debates up to the comm techs," Gidal finally said. "As long as they do their job and get me the important information, I guess the immediate need is being served."

"Local communication," I said. "That's what's important. It sounds like your printing project is doing the same kind of thing. I think I'd like to see one of your papers some time."

And by that, of course, I mean I'd have liked to fuck Gidal that evening. Under different circumstances, I probably would have.

Chapter 23. Campfire

When night started to fall, we set up camp. We opted for no campfire, because we were in unfamiliar territory, and the troublemakers tended to be very cautious about anything that might attract attention to us. The result was that we all sat in the darkness, with nothing but the moonlight to give us some indication of where to direct our gaze and speech as we conversed with one another.

Syck and Gidal were sitting together, speaking about previous campaigns they'd been on, although from simply over-hearing them I could not decipher whether they were talking about actual campaigns they'd been on or whether they were speaking of theoretical campaigns they'd like to carry out.

It made no difference to me; so far, I'd been impressed by their professionalism and, at least, the appearance of knowing what they were doing. I hoped I'd never need further proof than that.

The handyman finished up a meal and then came over to sit by me. She joined in my gaze, staring at the black horizon, not really able to see anything definite, but looking for shapes that could be something interesting or imagined to be something interesting. Mostly, I was just looking at the stars and thinking of all the strange noises they were sending down onto the Earth by way of the Godstream.

I sometimes imagined that the stars themselves pulsed in mathematical precision, and that they were sending equations to Earth in the Godstream, and that if someone would just sit down and pick out those equations and solve them, that all matter of heavenly secrets would be unveiled. And then other times, I wondered what the stars could possibly have to reveal to us. Probably not much.

I heard the handyman's voice, soft and private: "Have you ever heard of something called the Devnull?"

"I've heard the term, why?"

"You seem to know a lot about commie stuff, so I thought maybe you'd know what it was."

"Don't you?"

"I don't know what it is," she said.

"Neither do I."

As is often the case, when someone returns zero, the other person decides to fill in the information that they'd just claimed to be asking for. The handyman didn't disappoint me: "From what I can tell, it's a kind of void. Some place, kinda like...a black hole. A place where things go when they die, or where radio signals eventually end up once they've run their course."

The great Devnull, of course, was so much more than her rudimentary understanding. It was a living place of emptiness. A place that actually contains data, souls, history, knowledge, and more. So rich, and yet, we can never get to it. Some commies have theorized that there may be a way to reach into the Devnull and retrieve information from it. But if you reach into the Devnull and draw out information, then it was not the Devnull that you reached into.

The Devnull was something we had to accept on faith. There was no evidence of it, it had no frequency. You could not tune to a station and hear Devnull, or even the absence of Devnull. It simply existed, and contained everything that ever passed into it, and kept all of that well out of our reach.

Some day, we would all pass into the Devnull. After that, I know nothing more.

"It's like that," the handyman continued, pointing into the darkness in front of us. "Completely dark, full of information we can't quite make out. That's the Devnull."

"Sounds like that's static, to me," I said. "The Devnull, if it is what you say it is, would be even less than that. There would be nothing to point at, if you were pointing at the Devnull."

"Maybe," she agreed. "But that would mean that the stuff in front of us was that weird-sounding static I sometimes hear on the radio. With information we can almost hear and yet, not hear."

"That sounds about right," I agreed. "So how would it be, if something started putting little specks of light out there? or cut-outs of terrifying structures."

"Then we'd start thinking there were new stars, or new cities, or structures. We would think we'd learned something...but we wouldn't have learned nothing, really, because, it's being manufactured. It's faked."

"And now you know why Rkicr isn't such a smart commie," I said. "And you are."

The handyman was silent for a long time at being deemed a commie. I imagined that she already suspected I myself was either a commie or a commie apprentice, so there might have been some extra weight to the complement coming, as it had, from me.

"I'm no commie," she said. "Not yet."

"Well, you're something," I said. "I'm not sure what. I'm still trying to figure that out."

"What d'you mean?" she asked. "Heck, I'm still tryin' t'figure you out."

"I'm simple enough to understand," I said. "You're the one always talking about these commie ideas, and it was you who discovered the pirate station, and it's you with a secret bunker."

I looked over at her. I knew that even in the darkness she could sense my stare. She was silent for a while, and then finally said, "I ain't nobody, honest. I'm just a handyman, with a tendency to be, maybe, a little too curious for her own good."

"Nothing wrong with that," I admitted. "But if you have some piece of knowledge or a suspicion or anything that you haven't shared with me, I'd appreciate you telling me about it."

I felt her move closer to me until we were right next to each other. She said in a low voice, "I think Rkicr is in on this pirate station. And I think time's come for him to be replaced."

I was taking her at her word. I didn't get the sense that she was inventing these suspicions, because so far she'd done nothing but reveal new information that had been pretty accurate. I didn't know where she'd gotten her information -- maybe it was from curiosity as she claimed, or maybe she was receiving signals on her radio from some remote group, or maybe she'd been instructed by someone on what to do and what to reveal. Either way, she'd been right. A lot.

"Sounds like you want to replace Rkicr and will say anything to get his job," I said.

She ignored me, probably recognizing it as a bluff. "I think you were a member of the Children of Elektronix. I think you're a commie. I think you need to take over KCG station, before the pirate station and Rkicr manage to implement their campaign of disinformation or whatever it is they plan to do."

She had obviously been on the lookout for me from the moment I arrived at the farm. She was obviously a part of the Children of Elektronix, such as it was, whatever it was now.

I said, "I thought you seemed awfully well-equipped and over-informed for being a noob handyman."

"Naw, I am just a noob handyman. But I have a lotta friends, and we been lookin' for you, and a few others, too."

"Now," I said, "just who do you think I am? and what are you looking for me for?"

"Well I know who you are," she said. "You're Ender, otherwise known as Enid. So you were one of the original twenty-four, and you helped destroy, well, a good portion of the old world; the data center in KKT, the media centers in KTLA, the market in KNY, the holdouts in KVT and KMA..."

She went on and on, listing off every exploit I'd ever been a part of. And she knew each one. She added a few in, probably the stuff of legends; things I got credit for helping in just by way of association. So sometimes she was wrong, but mostly she was right. She was wrong about me being an "original twenty-four" because I was hardly original within the Children of Elektronix. But possibly the new Children of Elektronix based their existence off of the iteration I'd been a part of, and so to them, that was the original. It was, I guess, the original Children of Elektronix of the New World.

"So you're a member of this 'Children of Elektronix' group?" I asked.

"I am," she said, "And so is Gidal."

I looked in the general direction of Gidal and Syck to make sure we were still talking to one another and not listening to us. I wondered if she was lying; if I'd been her, I'd have lied just for the added effect, true or not.

"Well, count me out," I said. "I'm not looking for a new job. You take Rkicr's position at KCG. You're smart, you'll figure it out."

I didn't really expect that to go well, but figured I had to try. I waited for the obligatory gun in my side or knife at my back.

I was wrong, however, and no life-or-death threat was made. The handyman said, "Suit yourself. But if you want to keep the Godstream pure, you'll think about what I've said."

I put her words out of my mind, and we heard Gidal approach. He knelt down before us handed me something that my fingers vaguely remembered; it was paper. Real paper, thick and rough on my fingertips.

"You said you'd like to read something we'd printed," he said. "Keep that til daylight, if you want, and look it over. If you want."

"Thanks," I said, unfolding the paper in my hands and trying to tilt it so that it caught some moonlight. It was too dark, however, and so I stuffed it into one of the pockets of my pants. "I'll read it tomorrow. What is it?"

"An old document. They called it the Revolutionary's Catechism. No-one knows who wrote it, but we've been printing copies of it and distributing it for years now."

"This is the Revolutionary's Catechism?" I asked. The Children of Elktronix had spoken of its ideals and principles, and I'd heard that it had been based on a historical document, but I never imagined that anyone had the actual text of it.

The Revolutionary's Catechism was one of those documents that no one had ever actually read and yet everyone claimed to know. Even more, whenever anyone said anything vaguely profound or significant, they could always add to its weight by stating that it was a quote from the Revolutionary's Catechism. It was most certainly the stuff of legends, and so for a copy of it to surface now seemed highly improbable.

"This is the original work," he assured me.

"Or so you say," I said, skeptically. "This could just be a transcription of what people always attribute to it."

"It's the real thing," Gidal said. "I know it is."

Chapter 24. Auto-hut Village

At daybreak, I awoke and quietly stood, careful not to disturb the handyman who was still sleeping. Gidal and Syck had taken turns at night watchman duties; Gidal was on watch now. I felt my pants pocket, felt the paper, took it out to look at it.

The document appeared to be what he'd said it was; some old world, militant text, about a revolutionary's obligations and duties, and how all of their goals may be achieved. It read like any old document did; a foreign language with a built-in presumption that the world operated in some very specific way. Of course, back when the document was written, if it was in fact the actual Revolutionary's Catechism, the world did work a certain way, so it was right. But its very existence had altered the way the world came to function, and so it was, by being a catalyst of change, outdated by the change it instigated.

Even so, the idea of the document, the encouragement of strength and resolution in the face of injustice and lack of a sane social structure, had become a common and core belief in even the common people of this, the new world.

I read the document over once, then took it over to Gidal. He took the paper from me and put it into his own pocket.

"Did you read it?" he asked.

"I read it, just now," I said. "Strange to feel the paper you're reading right there, between your fingers."

"That's how they used to communicate," he said. "They wrote it down, and passed the papers around."

"And the only price was most of the world's woodlands," I said. "What a deal."

"Some people don't know the meaning of moderation," he said. "I think we've learnt that now."

"Let's hope so," I said. "Although it doesn't seem like this pirate station has. Is it safe to have a campfire during the day?"

"Keep it small," he said, "but I'd say it was OK. You gonna make breakfast?"

"I thought I might. And some coffee. You want some?"

"I think I'm sufficiently off night-watch now. I'll help."

We managed to make a small fire, and to boil water. We threw a couple of MRE's in the water until everything was well heated. Most MRE's contain instant coffee packets, so we stirred that into the water and had coffee.

At the smell of the coffee, the handyman awakened and joined us for breakfast. Syck was, perhaps, not a breakfast eater or was simply still tired from having taken the initial night-watch, because he didn't stir.

I waited for the two to start discussing Children of Elektronix philosophy or plans, but they simply ate and made polite conversation about how we all had slept and how nice the mountains were, and sipped our coffee, and prepared ourselves for another day of walking.

At the end of breakfast, we packed everything up, awakened Syck, who drank the last cup of coffee and wolfed down some food, and we were on our way.

After a few hours of walking, we reached the peak of a mountain, and as we crossed over to the down slope, we saw below a small village or encampment. The encampment consisted exclusively of auto-huts; old, decrepit automobiles converted into small homes. There was a road, more or less, running through the village, and most auto-huts had a yard or garden, many of them didn't even bother having tyres, so they'd all obviously been there for some time and had no intention of leaving. It was a settlement.

We stood at the peak of the mountain for a short while, looking at one another for some indication of mutual consensus.

"I say we walk right through it," the handyman said at last.

"So do I," I agreed. Looking at the weaponry Gidal and Syck were carrying, I added, "But we should probably be discreet about the fire power."

Gidal and Syck slung their rifles over their backs, leaving their hands empty of weaponry.

Taking their compliance and their lack of protest as agreement, we continued down the side of the mountain. As we walked, I moved ahead from Gidal and Syck, and as I'd expected, the handyman stuck close by my side. I said to her, "So what's this all about?"

"It's an auto-hut village, been here for as long as I've known the area. There's a friend we should talk to in a blue van up near the end of the road. He's kinda expecting us."

"How does he know to expect us?"

"He just knows that if I found you, then we'd come see him."

"OK. I guess we'll have a talk with him, then."

"He'll probably want to join us," she said. "If you're OK with it, I think he could be of help."

"As what? Troublemaker?"

"Call it what you will," she said. "He's got a lot of explosives."

"If this station has a radio station that can overpower KCG, I think the last thing we'll want to do is blow it up."

"Might be the only way to get it to stop broadcasting. Children of Elektronix always was willing to lose a hand to save an arm."

She was right. The people's militia and the Children of Elektronix both had been marvelously impractical in that way. Pragmatic "art of war" dictated that if an army was to discover a wealth of supplies, then they would not destroy it but instead take it all for their own use. Not the militia. They would destroy it. They destroyed everything that stood in their way, and what they hadn't destroyed, the Children of Elektronix had destroyed later, simply for representing the old world. That was crime enough, in their eyes.

We descended down the mountain until we reached the beaten path running through the settlement. A few people were still sleeping, others were either starting their mornings or finishing up their morning routines. A few stray dogs followed us as we walked. People generally gave us suspicious looks as we passed, not sure what to make of us. I guess we didn't look like cranks, although personally that would have made me all the more suspicious, were I in their position.

It occurred to me that maybe they weren't terribly suspicious of us simply because there'd been traffic lately anyway. If we were taking the most convenient path toward the pirate station, it could be assumed that everyone else going to and from that station would also take this path. For all these people knew, we were just more of the same.

A man working in his garden stopped what he was doing and looked at us as we started to pass his auto-hut. I decided to stop and chat.

"Nice place you all have here," I said. "Got a name for it?"

"Auto. Hut. Village."

The handyman laughed a little, as she often did when hearing something she found silly. Luckily he didn't seem to take offense.

"How long has this place been here?" I asked. "It looks fairly well established."

"A while," he said. "I mean, I been planting this garden for about eight seasons I think."

"Long time," I agreed, although I wasn't entirely sure whether there were one or two seasons in a full rotation around the sun. "I guess you don't get too many visitors around here."

"Yep, not really," he said. "Couple of travelers now and then. Maybe a transport ever so often."

"A whole transport?" I asked. "I wouldn't expect that."

"Oh, I imagine you would. I reckon they'd be going the same place you're going."

"We're not going anywhere in particular," I said.

"Well, we live by Berkley's Law here," he said. "You can claim a plot, put your auto down on it, and do what you want with it. There's no obligation to share nothin', but don't expect us to share nothin' with you, neither. Anything we do share, that's just bonus."

"We're not looking to settle down just yet, either," I said. "We're looking for work. We're techies, mostly, just looking to help out."

He shrugged, "I don't know much about tech."

"Nothing around here for a techie or a handyman?" the handyman asked.

"Not that I know of. You might ask Joe, down on the end, in the blue van. He likes technology, always got some gadget doing something I'll never understand...or care much about."

"We'll do that," said the handyman. Obviously Joe had been the man we'd intended to see anyway.

We continued through the camp, passing people in and out of their auto-huts, each with their own unique story and history. Some were playing solitaire and looked as if they probably never left the same seat in their auto-hut, others were tending to their huts, making random home improvements, one woman was hanging out laundry on a line, others tinkered with mechanics, others were talking and carrying on happily.

Joe was sitting on the floor of his blue auto-hut, tinkering with a number of radios, each in parts. When he saw us, he made no sign of recognition, but I'd have expected that.

"You Joe?" the handyman said.

"Who's asking?" he said.

"Some guy down that-a-way said you were a techie, and might know where there was techie work."

"Ya'll don't look like techies to me. You look more like a militia."

"Couple'a troublemakers decided to tag along," she said. "Can't get rid of 'em."

Joe laughed a little. "OK. Well, there obviously ain't nothin' goin' on around these parts. But if you go up a ways, I've heard there's a comm station there. I guess they'd need tech help for maintenance."

"We just came from KCG," the handyman said. "Rkicr was there, and he still is, but I'm pretty sure I found him a replacement if he wants to get out of the bizness."

At that, Joe set aside his radio project and gave us his full attention. "I see. The KCG station back up? I haven't been able to get a broadcast in a while."

"Nope, still something wrong with it," the handyman said. "Which is why I kinda thought maybe he was gettin' out of the bizness."

"Yup," Joe said. "Sounds like he might want to. Tell ya'll whut, I kin probably take you up yonder to the station, if'n ya'll want."

Syck stepped forward at that and said, "You know some of the people up there or you just want to tag along?"

"Just wanna tag along, maybe see if there's any work. I'm handy with wires and cables and stuff, myself."

"We don't need any extra people tagging along," Syck said, as much to Joe as to the handyman.

Gidal was watching us, saying nothing. I got the sudden notion that Syck was a liability.

"I don't see any harm in it," the handyman said. "We could always use a pair of extra tech hands."

Syck looked at me. I looked from him to everyone else. Obviously everyone knew what was really going on, except Syck. All he could see was an extra person to watch, and to be suspicious of.

"Syck," I said, "you got your ammo, and we've kept our side of the bargain. If you want to turn back now, we're fine with that. Otherwise, we're bringing Joe along. And if that's a security risk, then, maybe you should turn back to KCG. No hard feelings, nothing personal. We're just. I think we've got some new ideas about this trip."

Syck looked to Gidal, who simply looked back at him, as still as stone.

"I don't know what your new ideas are," Syck said, "but if I'm gonna go along with it, I'd like to know a little bit about what's going on."

"It seems everyone in this group is pretty much hell-bent on destroying the radio station," I said. "And then we're going to supplant the commie in KCG with a new commie, and none of that is open for discussion."

"OK, well, I was kinda hoping for that anyway," Syck said. "They don't call me a troublemaker for nothing, do they?"

Gidal smiled, and the handyman looked sufficiently pleased with Syck's answer. Joe had already grabbed a backpack full of some kinds of technical equipment which I could probably have named, although I had not yet seen. He closed up his auto-hut, locked its doors, and turned back toward us.

"Well if we're all straightened out, then, I guess that's all there is to it."

I was unsure of what kind of confrontation we'd just avoided, but I would soon find out.

Chapter 25. To Protect the Godstream

As we walked on for the rest of the day, Joe and the handyman and Gidal walked together often and spoke about whatever it was they spoke about. At first I assumed they were catching up with each other, on whatever they'd each been doing. Later I got the uneasy sense that they were discussing plans that might effect us all.

Syck said quite discreetly to me, "Is there something going on I should know about? You in trouble with these people?"

"Not me," I said, which I truly believed. "But don't think they don't have their own goals, and don't think I necessarily know what those are, because I don't think I do."

We came upon a pack of stray dogs at one point, looking unpleasantly hungry and possibly rabid. Gidal and Syck tried to scare them off from a safe distance, but they were ignored. Finally, Syck drew a handgun, took aim, and put a bullet through one of the sicker dogs' skull. Brains and blood splattered all around the pack of dogs, and they scattered.

When we reached the carcass, Syck kicked at it a little bit, looked it over. "Rabies or something. Not dogs you want to take home as pets."

"You could have just scared it away," I said. "You didn't have to kill it."

"I put it out of its misery is what I did," Syck said. "Besides, I thought we were gonna go blow something up. You think that's gonna just scare some people away?"

We continued to walk mostly in silence until afternoon. We stopped for lunch, perhaps staying longer than we'd intended, simply out of exhaustion. I'd been walking almost non-stop for days, and the others weren't used to walking this much, and today the sun was not being kind to us.

We talked a little about setting up camp then and there, simply because we weren't really in a great hurry, and we were all tired. But in the end, we went on simply because we didn't know how long the actual mission itself would take, or what the actual mission was yet. We only had so much food and water with us, so we decided that the faster we got finished with business, the better.

It was a good thing we kept walking, because with an hour, around a bend in the mountain path we were following, we encountered the first towering, terrifying, technological giant.

It was a huge, patchwork power relay. Cables stretched to it from a higher peak, and tangled its way through it, and then passed on to a tower farther along our path. Its metal stanchions were a tangled maze of crossbeams and rivets. It was rusty and loud, whining and sparking, humming with power.

Joe stopped dead in his tracks when he saw it. I couldn't tell if he was awe stricken by the ingenuity that had cobbled it together, or horrified at the amount of power coursing through it.

I said, "The comm station must be a pumping out a hundred thousand watts."

"Ridiculous," Gidal said.

"I believe it," said the handyman.

Joe nodded. Then he said, "We have identified a prime target, anyway."

We walked on, and as we walked dozens of similar towers emerged from the horizon. They were clustered together in some places, spread apart with cables that swung in the wind in others, they towered above us, they reached into the sky and disturbed our vision and minds. They were like scarecrows of old, only a hundred times as great, and alive with electricity.

We pressed on and found over the next ridge a farm of solar collectors and windmills. They were clearly recycled, not constructed by whomever owned the pirate radio station.

"These are left-overs from the old world," I said as we passed along the ridge over-looking the solar and wind collection field. "You can tell, from the design and manufacture."

"So maybe the station is a crime of convenience," Gidal said. "Someone discovered a field of power-collection, fixed it up or built up an array of relays, and then built up a radio station to utilize what they were harvesting."

"I wonder if the radio station was a found object or if it was constructed, or imported from some other place," Joe said. "I reckon we'll find out when we see it."

We kept traveling until we finally came into visual contact with the radio station and its surrounding community. It was far off, in the distance, just up on the peak of a mountain, with a trail of power relays and cables leading up to it along the mountainside. It was a grotesque, tentacled creature, resting hungrily on the peak of the mountain, sucking its life from the constructs below.

It was late, and so we decided to camp for the night, and make first contact in the morning. So we set up camp. The handyman and Joe volunteered for food duty

I said I'd scout the area just to ensure that we were in as a secure location as we could be when in foreign territory with every intention of destroying our ultimate destination. Gidal volunteered to go with me, citing his position as a troublemaker on the journey. I didn't argue.

As we scouted, Gidal said bluntly yet conversationally, "So you were with the Children of Elektronix, a while ago?"

"I might have been involved with them," I said. "I might not have been. Hard to say, when no-one ever admits who they are or what group they represent."

"Well you know me," said Gidal. "I mean, a little. I'm Gidal. And I do represent the Children of Elektronix."

"No you don't. That group disbanded a long time ago. So whatever you represent now might call themselves that, but it's not the same."

"It is the same," he said. "Some of us knew some of the original members."

"That doesn't mean it's the same. And if it is: why don't you tell me, what's your mission? What are you out to do that's so significant that you have to join a group with a fancy name to accomplish it?"

"We're out to protect the new world," Gidal said. "To protect the Godstream."

"What do you know about the Godstream," I said. "You people, you don't even know how to grep through a system log, much less what the Godstream is."

"The Godstream contains every bit of information we need to survive," Gidal said. "It has the history, the present, and the future in one signal. And that signal is eternal, from the sky, from nowhere. Do you want to know where the Godstream comes from? where it really comes from?"

"More than I can say," I said with a fair amount of biting sarcasm.

"The great Devnull," Gidal said.

I felt every fiber in my being tingle, and yet, my stomach twisted into knots. I couldn't bring myself to speak.

He waited for me to recover. He wasn't proud, he didn't seem to care that he'd just blown apart my entire universe. He was watching me, but he wasn't watching me spitefully or as a challenge.

Weakly, I said, "Impossible. Nothing can come out of Devnull."

But even as I said it, I realized I could not believe it completely.

When we got back to our little camp, the others were eating.

"Here's yer dinner," the handyman said to me, handing me a few packets of MRE food. I sat down and ate, but did not taste anything. I was too busy thinking about this idea, that the Godstream was a product of the Devnull. Or that they were products of each other, in perhaps an infinite loop of information and entropification.

The handyman gave Gidal some food and a thermos of coffee, "Made ya'll some extra coffee fer tonight's watch, if ya'll want it."

He and I ate, and the handyman made me some sweetened tea for dessert. Night fell, and she stayed close to me, talking to me about radio signals and things she claimed not to understand. Eventually we fell asleep, with Syck on the first watch.

In the middle of the night, I awoke to see Gidal waking Syck from having drifted off to sleep, and then taking his place as night watchman. Gidal looked in my direction, and watched me or the handyman or both, and then turned his attention back to the horizon. There was that faint city-glow at the peak of the mountain where the station lay. I could see his face faintly. He appeared calm, satisfied, confident.

I was not a noob. I was a commie. Someone would be dead by morning, this I knew.

Chapter 26. Devnull

> The revolutionary despises public opinion,
> despises and hates the existing social morality
> in all its manifestations. For the revolutionary,
> morality is everything which contributes to
> the triumph of the revolution. Immoral and
> criminal is everything that stands in its way.
> — The Revolutionary's Catechism

In the morning, I awoke, shaken by my mid-night suspicions. I tried to recall what I'd seen, or if I'd actually seen anything at all. I remembered Gidal's long stare over in my direction, and my heart skipped a beat. The handyman was laying on her side, turned away from me, and I grabbed her and turned her onto her back, examining her, feeling for a pulse, feeling her throat. This awakened her, of course, but she was calm as if she was always awakened this way.

"I couldn't hear you breathing," I said by way of an excuse.

"Thanks," she said. "I am breathin', aren't I?"

I smiled and nodded. "Sorry, I had a bad dream."

We got up and ambled over to make some food. I looked over at Gidal and asked, "Fire or no fire? Your call."

Gidal looked at the city ahead and shrugged, "We could risk it, but then again, why bother? We'll eat cold food this morning."

The handyman and I started preparing food for everyone, insofar as we could. There wasn't much to do for cold MRE's. The activity awakened Joe, however, and he was grateful for our offer of food.

After we'd all eaten, I went over to Syck to rouse him, and gave him a tap on the back with my foot. There was that kind of lifeless movement when I kicked him, that sort of movement that a body makes when the muscles are not themselves causing the movement in anyway nor automatically correcting for movement prompted by an external force.

I knelt down, knowing already that I'd been right, after all. I shook him, but to the touch he was nothing but flesh. It was like I wasn't touching Syck, I was just touching meat. Even so, I couldn't help but shake him, trying to rouse him, as if not believing that he'd gone into the great Devnull would make him return. But that wouldn't happen, of course. Nothing returned from the great Devnull. At least, not usually.

I stood and found the others staring at him in what did appear to be surprise. But I knew it was feigned. And so that was what we did; I pretended to not know that they'd killed Syck, and they pretended to not have killed Syck, and I pretended not to know that they knew that I knew they'd killed Syck, and they pretended to not know that I knew that they'd killed Syck. It was a bad child's game, maybe done for our individual protection from one another, or maybe because I hadn't seen them kill him, so there would always be that question, that uncertainty that they did.

"Is he..." Gidal said as he hesitantly approached the body, and he shook the body as I had, saying, "Syck, buddy? you OK?"

He examined the body a little closer, and then said, "He's dead?"

"Are there any marks?" the handyman said. "Any sign'a what happened?"

"Wasn't he OK when you relieved him of watch?" Joe asked Gidal.

Gidal said, "Yeah, he was alive and well, far as I could tell. He seemed a little tired but, nothing unusual. Well, actually he seemed right tired. Over-tired."

"He always was sleepin' real late, too," the handyman said. "That didn't seem quite normal. Wonder if he was sick. I mean, sick, like, ill."

The thermos of coffee that the handyman had made was lying on the ground near where they'd sat to perform their watch. I approached it, looked at it. Didn't say anything, just looked at it from where I stood.

"I got up. I guess it was around oh-two-hundred. Syck didn't say much, just, nodded and gave me a pat -- on the arm -- just like this --" Gidal went over to Joe and gave him a firm pat on the arm the way men do. "I, I sat down, had some coffee to wake up, and Syck, as far as I know, went to sleep. And that's all. No-one entered this camp site last night, at least not on my watch."

"We're not blaming you, man," Joe said.

I couldn't help but notice the blatant inclusion of how he'd drank coffee. I wondered if any of them would drink from that thermos now. I reached down and picked it up, opened it. It was, of course, empty.

The handyman went round to get a good look at Syck. She seemed repelled by the body, afraid to go too near it. But she made a cursory inspection with her eyes, and finally she said, "Either this man was ill and none of us knew about it -- possibly he didn't even know about it -- or some little insect living out here in the mountain got to him."

"Are we sure he's dead?" Joe asked. "Ain't there sicknesses that make you look dead? but you're not?"

By turns, we all shrugged. I said, "I think I've heard of things like that. But he seems pretty dead to me."

We stood in silence, not in reverence but in awkwardness, until Joe said, "You know he shot that damn dawg the other day an' then got real close to it. You don't think he caught somethin'?"

"From a dead dog?" Gidal said. "Nah...I don't think so. Well I hope not. Everybody else feel OK?"

"I feel OK," Joe said.

"I feel awright," the handyman said, looking suddenly uncomfortable. "But I don't like it. Let's get outta here."

We started walking until finally Gidal said, "Are we supposed to bury him?"

"It's unsanitary not to," I said. "I think. Or are you supposed to leave them out for the animals to git?"

We all tried to remember what we'd been told about sanitation and ecology. We all seemed to agree that burial or cremation, in populated areas was important. None of us could remember the rules for being out in wilderness areas where there was really nothing to pollute.

We ultimately decided that since we had no tools with which to bury him, and certainly could not risk a funeral pyre, and we didn't know if he'd caught something or not anyway, that we would simply leave him in hopes that some animals would happen along and devour the body.

Gidal didn't even take Syck's guns and ammunition. He'd been carrying no food or supplies to speak of but it seemed like normally you'd take what was left from a dead person rather than let it go to waste. I thought of going back to take the chain he'd worn around his neck, maybe wear it on my wrist as a bracelet. I just felt like I should take something to remember him by. Not that I'd known him that well, but it had seemed like such a waste.

I didn't go back, though. First because I wasn't sure why he'd died, and second because we were already walking. And I just had no reason to go back to remember him by. The thing lying back at that camp was nothing; going back and taking a token of remembrance would do nothing for Syck, because Syck was in the great Devnull now. He didn't care if I took something of his or not.

Maybe I'd hear him some day, in the Godstream.

"It doesn't seem like he had to die," I said aloud, to no one in particular.

They were all quiet, and Joe, being the newcomer with the least emotion invested into the venture, said for everyone, "Everybody dies."

We continued toward the radio station on the hill.

Chapter 27. Station

We only walked for maybe two hours before we were close enough to the radio station to consider ourselves seen and acknowledged. Approaching with a collection of guns wasn't the most subtle of ways to visit, so we considered also that we were probably considered a threat from the start.

The radio tower was surrounded by a small community, but it was a makeshift, haphazard city composed of sheet-metal shacks, auto-huts, and spare-part buildings. The radio tower itself was fairly well-constructed and probably had been revived from an old world radio tower. Most were, although this one had probably been one that nobody wanted to bother repairing. Whoever had implemented this tower had taken a lost cause and made it into an all-powerful broadcasting mothership.

As our arrival was utterly immanent, Joe asked, "Do we have a plan for this or we just wingin' it?"

"Ender always has a plan," the handyman said. She might have been sarcastic but I knew her too well. She was serious, and she was banking on me.

Gidal and Joe moved closer together and I could sense the backup plans being made, if only in facial expressions or physical proximity. I didn't care. The fact of the matter was that if this group of self-proclaimed rebels wanted this to go one way, they would make it go that way. It didn't much matter what kind of internal plans they were making. Such is the case with any number of people; you may call yourself a group or a team or a collective, but each person's will -- their true will, the one they themselves are not even aware of -- is unbend-able.

We kept walking until we reached the open entrance into the city. They did have a large set of doors there in the entryway to their little basecamp, but presumably they used these only at night. They didn't need it during the day because by the time we reached the gate and could have gone through, there were a dozen men standing outside their huts and buildings, each armed with two or three guns.

They were an ugly set of men. Few were shaven, few bothered with shirts, and most looked like they'd seen their share of action. It wasn't KCG, that's for sure.

I stood in the entrance with my hand on my revolver, pondering the men as they pondered me right back. I got the impression that they may have mistook me for a man because they lacked the sneer that men often get when a woman takes a stand.

"Ya'll lost?" the man closest to us said.

"Just out for a stroll," I said. "Saw a radio, thought you might need some techies."

"Ya'll're on private property," he said. "And we don't need no techies so go on 'bout your way."

"I guess we'll do just that, then," I said. "You know the nearest town 'round here? Someplace might be open to some newcomers?"

"Naw, there ain't no city 'round here," the man said. "You got a ways to go 'fore you hit any place with civilization. You musta seen the auto-village down there a ways, though."

"Not quite our type of place," I said. "Thanks anyway though. Mind if we pass through or you want us to go around?"

"Ya'll kin go on through," the man said. "I'm not sayin' you kin stop for lunch, I'm just sayin' ya'll kin go through."

We progressed into the encampment, and I could feel the tension in my companions. I could almost read their thoughts, see their worst-case scenarios of being surrounded by this group of cranks and robbed and probably killed. I hadn't gotten that sense, though, and I wanted to get a look at what they really had in their camp. It's easy to stand in front of a gateway with a few guns, possibly loaded, possibly not, and look mean. It was something else entirely to actually have enough supplies and weapons to back it all up.

The crank had made a mistake by letting us pass through, which was all I'd really wanted from the encounter after I saw they were not going to invite us in for a tour of the station. As we walked, I looked into the huts and buildings, few of which were really any more than immediate shelter from rainfall, and got a feel for how this group was living. And the answer was that they were barely scraping by. Whatever their goal was up on that mountain, they were achieving it but little else.

I believed the weapons they were carrying were pretty much all the weapons they had. The comm station itself, located near the tower, was the nicest building in the encampment, which wasn't saying much. It was completely enclosed and made of real materials, maybe transported there from afar or maybe recovered and repaired right where it stood. I knew radio stations well enough to know that there was not a hidden armory in the structure; it was too small to be concealing anything really significant. It was housing radio gear, I figured, and that was all it was housing. Maybe a few spare boxes of ammo, a few spare guns, but nothing serious.

That was my assessment, and I was hoping Gidal was getting an impression as well, rather than staring down the men we were passing. When we reached the opposite side of the encampment, we passed through its gateway and continued down the other side of the mountain.

"Thanks for nothin'," I said as we left.

"Same t'you," the crank said dispassionately, and watched us depart. And I could feel his eyes on us for at least a full hour as we walked away from the city.

Chapter 28. Plans

> This filthy social order can be split into several categories. The first category comprises those who must be condemned without delay. Comrades should compile a list of those to be condemned according to the relative gravity of their crimes; and there should be no delay in the completion of the task.
> — The Revolutionary's Catechism

Once we were far enough away from the city to feel comfortable talking, I said to Gidal, "What'd you think?"

"Dangerous," he said. "But all in all it ain't exactly a fortress. I didn't get the impression they were gonna let off easy, though."

"No, me neither," I agreed. "They were no militia, either, though."

"I find it doesn't really take a land cannon to stop me, mainly just a bullet or two would work," Gidal said.

"Well if you look at it that way, we've got that ourselves."

"There are a lot more of them than there are us," Gidal said.

"Yeah, shame Syck died, huh."

"Can't say, never really saw him shoot," Gidal said. "But yeah, the extra help would've been appreciated either way."

We walked in silence for a short while. I looked over at Joe, at the bulky backpack he had on his back and from which he'd never once drawn anything and might have never taken off for all I ever noticed. "Joe, what've you got in that magical weightless backpack of yours?"

"It ain't by no means weightless. But it could be magical. There's definitely enough bang in here to take down that tower and its station."

It sounded good, and it sounded to me like it was a pretty clear cut situation. Except for a few points that didn't quite seem to make sense, once you put the guns and ugly men out of the picture.

I said aloud, "Why would a bunch of cranks build a radio tower, and a station, and camp out by it, and all but pwn KCG's signal?"

The handyman gave me her thoughtful expression as she considered the question. Gidal and Joe had a more or less clueless expression, so I waited for the handyman.

She said, "They're protecting the station. They're hired hands."

That made sense. Every time the handyman opened her mouth, something sensible came out of it. I wondered how much she knew and how much she was really just guessing.

"Then somebody a lot smarter and a lot more purposeful is inside that radio station," I said.

"Well either way whatever they're doing is gonna have to stop," the handyman said. "So I don't understand why we care."

"Why does it have to stop?" I asked.

The handyman said, "Cuz it's interfering with KCG's signal. That's why."

"Do we know that? or are we assuming it? You said yourself you didn't like Rkicr so maybe he's just not broadcasting. How do we know what he's sending out? The guy could be nuts."

"I thought you checked?"

"I did, while we were standing right there in the station. The minute we walked out he coulda switched back over to static for all I know."

The handyman considered this. "Either way, I don't see how a rogue radio station is something we need to preserve."

She was right, and I knew it. But I also knew that she was withholding information, as I was. And I was pretty sure I didn't really want to walk back into a crank encampment with guns blazing and try to be the last man standing all over a useless comm station.

I was pretty sure the handyman knew who was in that radio station, and I was pretty sure that she wanted them stopped so she could supplant Rkicr at KCG. The relationship between those two, I wasn't clear on, yet.

I looked ahead and saw a nice, tall peak. I said, "Let's walk around that bend up there, and then set up camp. We'll be out of sight then."

Chapter 29. The Society

> The revolutionary despises all doctrines and refuses to accept the mundane sciences, leaving them for future generations. The revolutionary knows only one science: the science of destruction. For this reason, but only for this reason, the revolutionary will study mechanics, physics, chemistry, and perhaps medicine. But all day and all night the revolutionary studies the vital science of human beings, their characteristics and circumstances, and all the phenomena of the present social order. The object is perpetually the same: the surest and quickest way of destroying the whole filthy order.
>
> — The Revolutionary's Catechism

The Children of Elektronix had seen themselves as the product of an electronic age, with technology that had gone horribly wrong. They saw this technology as parent figures; like gods during your childhood, in whom you see no flaws until you become aware of how the world works, and then you see how the great potential of these mythical figures was never achieved. You see how weak they are, and you start to pity them and hate them all at the same time.

After the Revolution had happened, the Children of Elektronix formed as a collective of people dedicated to ridding the so-called New World of any sign of old world greed or mis-use of resources. These being largely subjective concepts, some of their targets were controversial both from within and outside the group itself. But the tendency was that one vote formed a consensus; if one person decided on a target, it was a target no matter what. It didn't matter if you didn't agree that it was worth being destroyed; if your comrade said that it was, then it was.

This served the group quite well during its brief lifespan. It meant that some of the largest vestiges of the old world were obliterated, and it also meant that small pockets of secret hold-outs that might have become a deadly old world virus to the new world ideas were weeded out.

I do not believe we were ever really wrong about the targets we chose. Not in the end. Not if the end was what we'd achieved. In that case, then the means were justified. I don't care what anyone said.

The broadcasts started making us out to be heroes and celebrities. Now, these were old broadcasts, before the commies took over the system, and so what one radio station broadcast, pretty much everyone in the world got to hear. So the Children of Elektronix didn't just get broadcast, they got famous.

Fame, as it happened, was one of the ultimate evils of the old world. It was the arbitrary selection of idols, and promotion of those idols to gods. When the Children of Elektronix itself became famous, it was a contradiction unto itself, and some of us saw that while others of us couldn't believe such a thing was possible. Some of the group believed that we had to be famous in order to get our ideas spread over the Earth. Because, apparently, our ideas were just that important.

Now, a fundamental belief in the new world was that things that are important don't need to be spread; they will develop independently and concurrent of one another. There was no belief system to spread in the new world; people would recognize the need to rid themselves of old world holdouts on their own. They didn't need a group with a fancy name to come around and show them how to do it, or even that it needed to be done.

That's why I'd left the group, and it was ultimately why the whole group had fallen apart. And it was, possibly, how the commies had really started to take over the system to abolish the global media. Local media survived, and regional media was implemented, but global media was suppressed. Because if we'd learned one thing from the old world, it was that sometimes, just because something is possible, doesn't mean it should be done.

Chapter 30. Camp

> The revolutionary can have no friendship or attachment, except for those who have proved by their actions that they too are dedicated only to revolution. The degree of friendship, devotion and obligation toward such a comrade is determined solely by the degree of their usefulness to the cause of total revolutionary destruction.
>
> — The Revolutionary's Catechism

That evening, the handyman and I went for a walk. I invited her on the stroll because I wanted her to let me in on her secrets. I doubted she intended to do that, but I figured giving her the chance to do so, safely out of monitoring distance of Gidal and Joe, would be a good idea.

So we walked down a few slopes and ended up sitting on a rock, watching the sun slowly descend behind the horizon.

"It looks like that comm station is going to be destroyed," I said to the handyman, "so why don't you tell me what's really going on. Starting with who's in the station; who's operating it."

"Wish I knew," the handyman said. "But I don't. Nor why they're doing it."

"So it's coincidence that you, Gidal, and Joe are all in the same revolutionist club?"

"And you are, too," she said.

"I'm not a member of any group any more," I said, and this was only marginally true for a few reasons. First, because you don't join a group like the Children of Elektronix and then just leave. There's not really an easy way out, because after you spend a week or two around those types of people, their ideas get into your own head, and they stay there, pretty much forever. And secondly because I'd gone from one group to another; so not only was I a lifelong member of the Children, I was also part of the commie brotherhood. There was not much you could do about it, I was a party member, with only slight variations in which party I claimed as my own.

"We're all dedicated to protecting some ideals," the handyman said. "This radio station goes against those ideals. You heard that crank, what he said: 'this is private property'. Not where I come from it isn't. It's GPL land, or it's Berkley's Law, or whatever, but only a crank or an old worlder would say something was private property. It was an affront to everything you ever did, and it's an affront to everything I stand for, too."

I stood, seeing that she was not going to give me any real information. She stood, as well. "You're in this with us, aren't you?"

"If I said no, wouldn't I wake up dead?"

The handyman looked genuinely hurt for an instant. "I'd hope you'd know the answer to that."

I did.

I turned to walk back toward the camp but her voice stopped me, along with her hand on my shoulder, gripping firmer than perhaps it should. "Let me see your back."

I stopped and sighed. "You don't need to see my back. You know what's there."

"I want to see for myself," she said. "Cuz no matter what you say at this point I won't know whether you're tellin' the truth or not."

"Same can easily be said of you," I assured her.

"Well I kin tell you trust me an' all," she said. "But I think it's only fair I should see if you got a scar or not. I mean, Bill did tell us that you did. And you said you didn't. I'd just like to know who's lyin'."

I smiled to myself because it no longer mattered whether I had a scar or not, but I could tell that in her mind, a gash in my back would be proof, part and parcel, that I'd been a heroic member of a militant revolutionary subgroup.

I took my shirt off, and lifted the back of my tank-top up so she could see most of my back. I could feel her eyes upon me, tracing the deep lines of the scar from the shoulder down.

"Just missed your spine," she said. "You're lucky t'be alive."

"I guess," I said, but that's not really how I felt about it.

I noticed she didn't ask why I'd lied or pretend to be hurt that I'd blatantly deceived her. Some people tend to think that there are unspoken understandings between people, that at some point in their relationship they can take things for granted about one another, like there was some common agreement. For instance, someone might think that the handyman and I had silently agreed that lying to one another and withholding information was acceptable.

This, however, is not true. It may never be true. People don't have silent understandings or unspoken agreements. They simply collect data about one another, for probably their entire lives. Some times one will make assumptions about the other, and often they will be right, but sometimes they are wrong. And often times, the time they are wrong is the time that it really matters.

This was a much larger issue than a simple relationship between two traveling companions, or even to techs, or even two lovers, or family members. It is something you will encounter with anyone you meet. They have notions of what you will be like, how you will behave. They will treat you in the way they feel appropriate, dictated by these beliefs they already have about you.

It was like the old handshake. You shake hands, and you can trust each other. Now we didn't have handshakes, but we still had these false unspoken understandings; these notions that we know someone.

The only way to find these beliefs out is, of course, to let the person tell you themselves. Since most people can't stand silence, the way to prompt them to tell you is by not saying anything at all.

These were commie beliefs and techniques.

We returned to camp and we all ate together. There was some discussion of how night watch was going to be handled. Joe volunteered to take the second watch, and I made a few polite offers myself. I could just barely sense their presumptuousness; I was just a woman, how could I stand watch? Joe ended up insisting that he was the right candidate for the job, which was fine with me. I would be the woman in need of sleep, and too inexperienced to stand watch, and a loyal and trustworthy companion. That suited me just fine.

We went to sleep fairly early. I slept lightly, and at around two in the morning I awoke, probably expecting Joe to be taking his turn as night watchman. However, I found instead that Gidal was sitting in position, asleep, and Joe was lying where he'd fallen asleep, still sleeping. Joe wasn't used to this sort of thing, obviously, and either Gidal hadn't tried to awaken him, or else Joe had indicated that he would awaken and had then fallen back to sleep and Gidal had done the same whilst waiting on him to take over.

Either way, I sat up slowly, quietly. Then I leaned over the handyman and kissed her forehead, gently stroking her hair to awaken her. I did this to avoid startling her into a loud and rude awakening. She stirred, and once she was lucid, I put my finger to my lips to indicate silence. She quietly sat up and then we both stood. I took hold of my backpack and weapons, and I took Joe's magical backpack. It was heavy as I'd expected, but manageable. The handyman had already gathered her things, and so we both set off, back toward the radio station encampment.

Chapter 31. The Plan

> It is superfluous to speak of solidarity among revolutionaries. The whole strength of revolutionary work lies in this. Comrades who possess the same revolutionary passion and understanding should, as much as possible, deliberate all important matters together and come to unanimous conclusions. When the plan is finally decided upon, then the revolutionary must rely solely on himself. In carrying out acts of destruction, each one should act alone, never running to another for advice and assistance, except when these are necessary for the furtherance of the plan.
>
> — The Revolutionary's Catechism

We walked toward the comm station silently for a long time, until we were well out of range of our former companions. Even after that, we walked in silence, until finally the handyman said, "Do you have a plan or are we just wingin' this?"

"We're gonna find out who's in that station and why," I said. "Because ultimately this is commie business."

"I told you you were Ender," the handy man said a little triumphantly.

"I didn't say I was Ender," I pointed out, "but this is commie business. And you and I are the two closest things to commies in this group. I need you to set explosives while I talk to them, whoever 'them' ends up being."

"You think they'll give us a chance to talk?" she asked.

"It'd be nice."

We continue walking. When we got close enough to survey the encampment, we found that three men were on patrol around the perimeter. There was that element of danger in my life that

I hadn't missed. No, I hadn't missed that at all. Getting shot for attempting to blow up a radio tower. It seemed so pointless now. Things like that had seemed very important at one time, but mostly, I think, because of the group mentality; when you have a small militia, it's easy to tell each other that it's normal to risk your life for an abstract cause. As one or two people, it's a lot more difficult to sustain that illusion.

I could see how it would have been done. Hide until there was a chance to get into the camp. Hide again until the guards passed by a second time, so you didn't make any further noise. Run to the radio tower. Freeze for the guards passing again. Put down an explosive and the freeze for the guards. Another explosive, freeze, another explosive, freeze, and so on. Then start back. Freeze. Continue. Freeze. Hide and freeze, then run away, and then trigger the explosion. Simple as that; it would have only taken three or four hours of continued, terrifying heart-pounding, adrenaline-pumping suspension of fear and reason. And then it would be over. Maybe. Maybe you'd fail, and your back up would have to do it. Or maybe you'd fail and you'd just trigger the explosives just before you sank into the great Devnull.

I couldn't do it. Not any more. I liked my mountain peak, I liked my Perch and my repeater tower and my konsole and my view of the world. I even kind of liked humanity, in the sense that we were trying now to live the right, justifiable, sustainable way. I had no desire to die, or to get too close to death.

So I sat down on the ridge where we were, and I said, "We'll wait until daylight."

"Daylight?" she asked.

"I'll go back in, in the morning, and see if I can talk to the commie there. While I'm doing that, you set explosives, just in case. Otherwise, I talk to the commie, and get things sorted out."

"What makes you think you can just talk to this guy and sort things out? Whoever it is, he's got cranks guarding the station.

He's not lookin' to be convinced that he should shut down his station."

"If he's a commie, then we owe it to him. Commies don't just go blowing each other up." I said it with extra solemnity and indignation in hopes that it would sound like a "commie code of honour" sort of rule. Of course I'd just invented it that moment.

The handyman considered something privately for a few moments, and then said, "His name is Memwatch. Him and a few others met on the radio at some radio-meetups that the Children of Elektronix held."

"When did they hold these?" I asked. "Ender never heard of it."

"That's because they did it on the Godstream."

I was silent.

She could feel the weight of my silence, and so she was fidgeting a little. She said, "Well it weren't my idea, believe me. But they done it, and the Godstream...scrambled it or encrypted it or whatever. So then they got the idea, let's start doin' some other stuff on the Godstream, kinda riding that wave I guess."

"And what," I said, "are they doing now?"

"Global information network," she said. "They figured on buildin' a global network on top'a the Godstream, so the commies could communicate all over the world, and the broadcasts could reach everyone. They decided that local and regional communication is too limited."

"How sure are you about this?" I asked.

"I know for sure about Memwatch," she said. "I know for sure about them piggybacking on the Godstream. And I'm pretty suspicious of Rkicr."

"Rkicr's signal is the one being overpowered," I said. "Why would he be complacent?"

"He ain't bein' overpowered. He's cutting his own signal so he can send out Godstream to other commies. It's a joint effort to get this system bootstrapped, and then everything goes back to normal. Except that everyone's also relaying the addendum to the Godstream."

"Then they'll be expecting us," I said. "They always were. Meaning..."

I stood up as the horrible realization struck me.

"Meaning what?" the handyman said.

Speechless, I took a few dazed steps back toward where we'd left Gidal and Joe as if those few steps would magically enable me to see their camp. But I was staring into nothingness, for a reason. I was staring into the great Devnull.

"Meaning what?" the handyman asked again, more firmly.

"They've sent cranks out that way," I said. "If they didn't kill us when we arrived, it was only because they didn't know what to expect from us. They were waiting for a safe time to attack."

"No," the handyman said. "No, that's not right. And if it is, Gidal and Joe can take care of theirselves."

I hoped she was right. I had nothing against Gidal or Joe, even if they did kill Syck, which I wasn't exactly positive about, although realistically I was pretty sure. But that didn't mean I wanted a bunch of cranks to sneak up on them and kill them in their sleep.

My resolve strengthened, then. There was no way to be sure if Gidal and Joe had just been sacrificed to this cause, but on the off chance that they had, we had to make sure it wasn't in vain. It was an old idea; death for death, kill for killing. It was an old world idea that was supposed to be beneath us. But in a sense, it was exactly what the Children of Elektronix had always been about; recompensation for a history of cruelty and oppression.

Those were poetic ways of justifying horrible acts, though. If you stood on the peak of a hill and shouted that out angrily, even in your own mind, then you could do anything and never give it a second thought. You could toss away every ethical ideal you ever had held precious, with total absolution.

And in your own mind, it's entirely possible to march into a crank's encampment and plant explosives, dodge gunfire, and decimate the buildings and people. It only takes a few moments in your mind, and there is no regret.

I looked over at the handyman, and I realized in that moment that I felt for her, very much, and her ideals and her beliefs and her pointless life goals. And I knew that if anyone was going to literally destroy the radio tower, it was going to have to be her, because I couldn't do it any more. I was past the point of blowing things up, risking my life even for retribution.

Chapter 32. Memwatch

> When a list of those who are condemned is made, and the order is given, no private sense of outrage should be considered, nor is it necessary to pay attention to the hatred provoked by these people among the comrades or the people. Hatred and the sense of outrage may even be useful insofar as they incite the masses to revolt. It is necessary to be guided only by the relative usefulness of these executions for the sake of revolution. Above all, those who are especially inimical to the revolutionary organization must be suppressed; destruction will produce the utmost panic in the government, depriving it of its will to action by removing the cleverest and most energetic supporters.
>
> — The Revolutionary's Catechism

Morning came and I shook the handyman out of her half-sleep. The sun was just coming up over the mountains, and the encampment was coming slowly to life for its final day of existence.

She and I had a little something to eat, although I think we were both too nervous really to eat much. I was upbeat and cheerful to make her forget about her nervousness, but my own was very present, deep down, and I kept thinking about what we were about to go do.

"Nobody came back into the camp last night," I said. "Meaning either they're still walking back, or they're dead, and Gidal and Joe are probably out looking for us. Either way, we only have so much time to get this done, so, let's get it done so we can have lunch and get ourselves back to civilization."

"Let's do it," the handyman said, hefting the backpack full of explosives onto her back.

We parted ways; I myself headed straight for the back gate of the encampment. About a million stories were floating around in my head, bullshit stories about how I'd escaped the crank assassins, how I was a commie, a sympathizer, an old world terrorist, how I'd been sent my Rkicr to stop the maniacs in the party I'd been with...I hadn't settled on any of these cover stories, and I knew I wouldn't until I was right in front of the gate. That's the way I operated. I chose my lie in the moment, and then in that moment, I believed it completely, with all of the back story and history I'd been developing subconsciously the entire time.

In order to lie successfully, your lie had to be the truth to you. This requires a great suspension of disbelief. Frequently the most successful method of achieving this is to simply split yourself into two parts; one part must be the trusting, unquestioning, innocent student and the other part must be a completely authoritative, all-knowing, clever teacher. The student must ask the teacher for the truth, and the teacher must tell that student everything.

I reached the back gate and stood before it as the cranks inside began to open it, having seen me approaching. In those few moments, the teacher told the student everything that had happened for the past five sunrises and sunsets. The teacher told the student names, places, events. And the student took it all in unquestioningly, and in that moment, that was all I knew in the whole world. Truly, in that moment, if you'd asked me about the handyman, I'd have honestly looked at you blankly and said, "What handyman?" I knew this feeling of rebirth; I'd done it many, many times before. And each time, it felt safe, and secure, and refreshing.

The gate opened and I was greeted by a group of cranks, well armed and very suspicious. I could see the fear in their eyes. This is how I knew that I'd been right; they'd sent a team out to kill us, and the fact that I was here, now, meant that their team had been killed.

"Mission accomplished," I said, which of course could have meant anything. "So I'd like to talk to Memwatch now."

The cranks might have had fear in their eyes but they weren't intimidated. They could have shot me then and there, and I was painfully aware of that. I didn't see any reason to hide my own fear, so I know I must have looked and sounded nervous. Because I was.

"You wanna see what?" one of the cranks asked.

"Memwatch, your radio operator."

They didn't respond.

"The commie," I said. "You can tell him Ender's here."

"Where's the rest of your party?" a crank asked. "What'd you come all the way back here for?"

"I'm here to talk to Memwatch," I said. "You tell him Ender's here."

"There ain't nobody here by that name, or title," a crank said. "I don't know what you think is goin' on here, but you come to the wrong place. Maybe you're lookin' for KCG, they got a comm station there."

"OK, I tell you what," I said. "I'm gonna go sit over there, on that hill. You tell whoever's operating your fancy radio tower, there, that Ender's here to see him. And if there's really nobody in that radio station, then when night falls, I'll walk away from here and never come back."

By this time the lie had set so firmly in my mind that I was feeling quite confident. I'd forgotten that I was nervous, that I didn't like the idea of dying. In fact, I was starting to crave a little danger, the threat of death. I'd been reborn into my lie, so what did I have to fear? The illusion was taking hold.

"You ain't going nowhere," one of the cranks said. He was the one with the obligatory authority problem.

"Just you tell him, alright?" I said, and walked away with complete confidence. They could have shot me in the back or attacked me or whatever they wanted to do, but when someone walks away from you the way I did, you just didn't do that.

I figured I'd bought the handyman some time. Enough time, if she was fast, to get most of the explosives set. I'd encouraged them to go talk to Memwatch, so my motive was clearly set. Of course none of them were moving to talk to the commie, but I didn't need them to do that.

As I walked, I turned, and said, "Anybody got a gun I could borrow?"

Some cranks ignored me, others laughed, but they all mostly hung around the back gate to see what wacky antics I had in store.

"No, really," I said. "I know a trick or two with a gun. 'Sides, I lost mine in a struggle a ways back."

That changed some of their moods, each of them wondering whether we'd defeated their assassins or whether I'd simply escaped.

"What kind of trick?" one asked.

"I can shoot a bullet straight into the air so it comes straight back down and hits a target on the ground," I said. "Really. I can point a gun at the sky, just so, and fire off a shot. And it goes way up high, and then straight back down. I have to move out of the way just so I don't shoot myself in the head."

One of the cranks took out a handgun and emptied it of all but one bullet. He held it out to me.

I walked back toward them and took the gun.

"You stand back, now," I warned them. "What've we got for a target?"

The men searched for something with which to create a makeshift bulls-eye. We finally decided on an empty can. It was a large can, one of the big serving sizes from the old world meant to serve a whole group of people beans or roasted peppers or some such processed food like that.

We set that down on the ground and I moved myself into position, carefully calculating the angle of the shot. I knelt down near the can and laid down on the ground, gun in hand and hand on the bean can lid. I looked up at the sky, staring into the empty blue, and the white fluffy clouds above us all. For a few moments I forgot where I was, and when I came back to, I looked around and saw almost every crank in camp at the back gate, waiting to see me either kill myself or perform a marksmanship feat equal only to William Tell.

"I'm not staying here," I warned them. "No way I'm getting that bullet through my head if I miscalculate."

They leaned forward as I made my hand firm and took aim.

I squeezed the trigger, felt my wrist, twisted as it was, jolt in pain from the back kick, and the explosion from the camp bursting into the blue sky, and around the cranks, and through the cranks. I rolled out of the way and ran like hell.

Chapter 33. Hellfire

I don't know what happened to half of those cranks, I don't know if they came looking for me or if they all died or just ran in the other direction. I assume some of them died, others ran, maybe some pursued me but by the time they recovered from the confusion, I must have been a mile away.

The way it had happened was, of course, that I'd seen the handyman lurking behind the hill when I was walking away from the back gate. Obviously she'd finished setting the explosives, and if she hadn't, then there was going to be a spectacular explosion for no good reason and not in the right location. But, having complete faith in my team member as you were supposed to have in operations such as these, I turned back to engage the cranks in what was, essentially, a death wish.

A death wish. I had them from time to time, mostly when I felt too nervous to do something simple and direct; in these moments, I tended to make things more elaborate, somehow hoping it would all go horribly wrong but somehow that in going so wrong, it would make everything turn out right. Since both of these -- "wrong" and "right" -- were subjective terms meaning opposite things to me and my enemies, it was really just a way that I left everything up to the Godstream. In its randomness, the natural patterns of the world would be revealed. Things would happen the way they were "supposed to" happen.

And so I put on a childish show, waiting for someone to think that I might be providing a distraction for some terrible deed. But of course at that point, I wasn't. I'd already distracted them; the deed was done. All that was left was the pulling of the trigger. So to speak.

So I got one of them to give me a gun, and we searched for a completely meaningless target for this frivolous magicians trick. And I got onto the ground and disappeared for a few moments, and while I did this, my hand automatically found its way into my pants pocket where the radio control was located, the one that would set off the explosives.

And at the precise moment that I pulled the trigger, I pressed the radio control button to ignite. And probably on the very Godstream itself, the radio signal traveled over my body, around the cranks, through their encampment, and into the receivers on the explosives.

The tower, we could see from a safe distance after we'd stopped running for our very lives in total abject fear, was in pieces and the electrical fire that had consumed it had fairly well melted every piece of metal and electronics into one big twisted mass. It was like a modern sculpture commemorating the greed of the old world. The building that had been next to it didn't really exist at all except as particular matter; it had been made of cheap cement, and so the few explosives that the handyman had set at its base had pulverized the entire building.

Explosions, in real life, are violent events that leave little standing afterwards. If any of the people in that encampment had come out of that area alive, they probably were badly burned, or cut by shrapnel, or crushed by pieces of building and radio tower parts. It was not something I was proud of, that part. But then again, I'd been taught not to think of that. The objective had been met. The gates of hell, created.

The handyman and I were sitting behind a hilltop, far from the encampment, watching for anyone approaching over the landscape, but it remained empty.

The handyman was dazed, more so than I. At least I'd known what to expect. At least I'd seen structures decimated by explosives I myself had set. At least I'd felt, and learnt not to feel, the impact of knowing that what you'd just done snuffed out the lives of a two dozen real people.

She was speechless, and so was I. So we just sat and looked.

Finally, after a long while, the handyman said, "I hope I don't see nobody coming after us. And I hope to Godstream I don't see nobody crawling out of that camp. I don't know what I'd do, then. What do you do? You go and help them? or you just let them...suffer?"

I frowned, recognizing those questions. I said, "You'd better not look any more, then."

She turned her back on the encampment, and I watched it simmer down into a blackened, useless, dead pile of debris.

We waited until we'd both recovered from having run for so long and so far, and then we continued walking toward KCG, changed women.

"You know," I said. "Your little group is a lot like the old world that they claim they want to destroy."

She didn't argue.

Chapter 34. Return to KCG

The first day of the journey back to KCG was uneventful. We were fairly quiet, the both of us, not so much for introspection but simply because we had nothing, in those moments of return, to say. What was there to say? The reason I'd left my mountaintop had now, more or less, been solved, and there was only a few loose ends left to resolve.

That was something worthy of discussion, but we didn't talk about it for the first day back toward KCG. But we both knew, in the back of our minds that we would be obligated by our own compulsion to deal with Rkicr. His original crime, of diverting his broadcasts, was a simple matter in comparison to his new crime; he'd been the root cause by both association and by simply lying to us, in our going all the way to the radio station, and becoming murderers.

You could say "soldiers" or "militia" if you wanted it to sound more socially acceptable. But you find it hard to reinforce this in your mind without a group around you telling you over and over that this is the truth, or a drill sergeant from the old world US Army threatening to rape you if you dared doubt it were so.

So we were just two aimless women, walking back toward KCG with three fewer people in our party than those that were along with us, and we'd done something that we'd both have to relegate to nightmares and secret thoughts that no one would know but ourselves.

"KCG is gonna need a new commie," I said to the handyman on the second day, as we neared the city again.

"Yep," she agreed. "I reckon there's gotta be somebody in the city that'll want that job."

"I kinda thought you might go for it," I said. "We could use a good man there, someone who knows the score."

"I'm not a commie," she said. "I'm just a handyman."

"You're a commie now," I said.

We walked in silence for a ways, and then she spoke up again. "What, just like that? What do I do, pick a name for myself and take an oath? Ain't there some kinda tattoo or something?"

"Nope," I said. "Just log into the konsole and start learning it. And broadcast like you're obligated to. That's about all there is to it, I'm afraid. It's how I learned. Heck, it's probably how must of us learned."

"So you are Ender," she said.

I didn't care about admitting to her who I was now. After you'd killed a dozen people together, you tended to care less about the small details.

"You mean you were bluffing the whole time?" I asked. "You never were really sure?"

"One thing about you," she said, "I don't know what to believe around you."

"Get used to it," I said. "The commies like to think they have that market cornered but really everyone's pretty good at it, they just don't lay claim to it. And anyway, you're not so transparent yourself, you know."

"Thanks I guess," she said. "Are we expecting Rkicr to just up and resign? because if he doesn't, I'm no good to you."

"He won't have a choice. Word's gonna spread of what he tried to do, whether or not he steps down from the position. In the end his reputation as a commie is gonna be useless, and he'd have to step down soon anyway. It's just how the commies work."

When we arrived in KCG again, we went to the same inn, found some space to settle in, and went downstairs for a meal and a drink. Dave was nowhere to be seen, which was a bit of a relief to us both. I think we were still contemplating how to tell Dave that both of the troublemakers he'd recommended to us were dead, whereas we were both alive. Then again, I wondered how familiar Gidal and the handyman were with one another, or for that matter, Dave and the handyman. It had hardly been coincidence that the handyman and Gidal were aligned with whatever group they mutually shared between them. The Children of Elektronix, maybe, or, more likely, some group calling themselves that.

We had dinner there at the inn, and when at least we became too tired to sit and make idle conversation, we decided to go back upstairs to get some sleep and reconvene tomorrow and deal with the rkicr problem.

We both went upstairs to the main sleeper room, and found that there upon the beds were sitting Gidal and Joe.

Chapter 35. Children

> The new member, having given proof of
> complete loyalty not by words but by deeds,
> can be received into the society only by the
> unanimous agreement of all the members.
> — The Revolutionary's Catechism

I stood in the doorway for a long time, not clear on whether Gidal and Joe had hunted us down in order to take revenge on us for having left them to be ambushed, or whether they were simply there for an emotional reunion, or whether there was a third intention altogether. The handyman was clearly far more confident, and she went into the room and sat on a third empty bed, and I got the sudden feeling that I was standing in front of the new Children of Elektronix, pound for pound.

Gidal spoke first, "What a long journey there and back again. So much has happened in so short a time. Strange how it works that way, sometimes."

I was still scanning the area, as casually as possible, for some sign of weapons. Could it have been possible that they hadn't intended for the mission to succeed?

The handyman said, "I been a fan of yours for a long time, Ender."

"Don't call me that," I said. "My name's Enid."

"Not to me it's not," she said. "Joe here's monster-b - you know, from KDE."

I did know the commie name monster.B. It was true that he was in charge of the comm station over in KDE, and of course I'd talked with him in the konsole. He was one of the more paranoid and perhaps "militant" of commies, known to those who'd talked to him enough as a good commie with, perhaps, a cruel and careless sense of justice, which was the commie way of saying politely that to make monster-b mad was to wake up one morning to find that your konsole has been set to a foreign character set, or worse that your archive tapes have been scrambled - not completely but just enough to provide you with a few days of work re-ordering the data. I'm sure he'd done worse to non-commies. Most commies had.

"And Gidal here is maddawg," the handyman said. "And I'm just plain old Ana Molly."

Maddawg was the commie from KAS; I'd spoken with him via konsole here and there but mostly knew him from eavesdropping in on his convo's with other commies, like Joe, aka monster-b. I knew he'd been friends with monster-b, that much came through in their conversation, and their political and commie views were clearly aligned.

"Ana Molly", as the handyman called herself, I'd seen from time to time on the konsole as well. I'd never really known who or what she was, but again she was someone who'd talked with monster-b and maddawg and a few other similarly-minded commies. I'd always assumed she was a commie just outside of our region, or an apprentice to some local commie.

I wondered if they were telling the truth or not, and if not, then what they had to gain from lying.

"How does all of this relate to Rkicr?" I asked. "Because I assume ultimately, it does."

I also was assuming that it all related ultimately to me, too.

"Very much so," Gidal said. "Rkicr is, just as you and Ana ascertained, the leader of a small movement within the commies to take over the Godstream. And we can't allow that."

"Then how does it relate to me?" I asked. "This has all been obfuscated too well for me to believe it's a happy coincidence that we're all meeting here."

"Children of Elektronix," Gidal said.

"You may not know this, but you're the only surviving member," Joe said. "And you almost got yourself killt back there by stealin' our stuff and goin' on the mission alone."

"What do you mean 'the only surviving member'?" I said, a little stunned.

"After your group disbanded, you went off to where ever you went, but the rest of the group stayed in KNY, I guess. Well, I guess they hadn't quite disbanded, really. It didn't make the broadcasts, but the building they were holed up in to re-configure the organization, was raided by local militia. Nobody survived."

I thought about this for a while. It made sense; after all, they'd done a lot of crazy things in their time, and after they started taking credit for the acts and taking silly old world style interviews on special broadcasts that, happily, the commies killed when they took over the airwaves, the group had become infamous. I could imagine a local group deciding that they were basically no more than a local street gang, and putting a stop to it.

"OK," I said.

"Some of us were helping out with the organization back then," said Gidal. "That's mostly how I became both a troublemaker and a printer. So me and Joe and a few others, we got a pretty good idea of what the group was all about."

"And we heard a lotta stories about you," Joe assured me.

"Most of them were probably not true," I said.

"There needs to be some group dedicated to preserving the new world ideals," the handyman said. "You know it's true, you've thought about it, I know ya have."

I said, "I'm here for one reason, and it's the same reason as I was here from the beginning; I just want to fix the broadcasts.

Once that's done, I'll be going back to my repeater tower and continue on as before."

"That's all we want you to do," Joe said. "What'd you think, we were here to enlist you into a militia?"

"You wouldn't be here to convince me to do something I already intended to do," I replied.

Gidal smiled a little. "OK, well there is one thing we need from you. We need you to transmit our messages, encrypted and as quietly as possible, without asking questions."

So they were forming an internal network. Basically the same thing that Rkicr and his friends were attempting to do, only instead of transmitting along with the chaos of the Godstream, this group wanted to transmit within a trusted network of known safe nodes.

"What will these messages contain?" I said.

"You'll be free to read them," Joe said. "They'll be encrypted using an old method of encryption; shared keys."

He obvious didn't see the look of recognition on my face that he wanted, which made sense, as I hadn't ever really had formal commie training. Not that there was such a thing anyway. He explained: "Think of it like a lock and a key; you'll have the key but no lock. We'll send you the lock; and as long as you're really you, then you'll have the key, and you'll be able to unlock the message and read it and then pass it along. Now if your tower gets taken over or if someone like Rkicr were to intercept the message, then that person would have the lock but no key. Get the idea?"

I nodded. I'd heard of these encryption methods but never knew them to be implemented in the new world. Each key was private; it would have a password known only to the individual commie, preventing anyone from using this key but that commie. It was one of the most secure forms of encryption and had literally been banned in the old world at different times, so effective it had been in disguising communication between people. Not everyone liked that degree of privacy back in the old world.

"And people only get a key if we meet them in person," the handyman added.

I felt my heart skip a beat. Travel. Seeing the world. Recruiting for a better commie collective. It was an appealing job offer if I could score it.

"For that you'll need someone trusted to go around to other commies, talk to them, verify their identity and their sympathy, and give them their own private key."

They all nodded, more or less simultaneously. I believe we were all thinking of the same thing.

"Then rather than guaranteeing my complacency with your plan, I'd like to volunteer to be your ambassador," I said.

"We were kinda hopin' you'd say that," the handyman said. "Everybody knows Ender, and everybody knows you can trust Ender. So you're the perfect candidate."

I shrugged, because that was always a safe way to admit and deny nothing, all in the same non-verbal gesture. I privately believed that they over-estimated my influence and notoriety, but then again, maybe I was under-estimating it.

"In that case," monster-b said, and then, referring to the handyman's commie name: "anomaly will return with you to your repeater station. You learn her all the things you do there and how to be a good 'n reliable commie, and when she's settled in, you go spread the good word."

"What about Rkicr?" I said.

Gidal rolled this thought around in his mind, you could see him doing it like someone might contemplate a taste of real coffee after a long journey. Then he said, "What about Rkicr. I think that's a problem that's been solved. Frankly, if he manages to implement his abuse of the Godstream, then let him. It won't affect us, not if we build an infrastructure. We can send out the pure Godstream with encryption, and we'll figure out how to decode his messages in his adulterated version of the Godstream with only a little bit of effort."

"The object isn't to destroy all the competition," Joe said. "It's to make sure we have a way to hold this infrastructure together. Our work is ultimately too important to leave up to chance. We need a network of trust, so we can broadcast reliable and verifiable messages to the regions that need the information. That's what we commies have always done, and it's what we'll continue to do."

"Information is power," the handyman intoned. It had been a cliche she'd heard on an old broadcast, I think.

"Do no evil," I said, also quoting a old and meaningless phrase from a long-gone information broker. It was funny how old world organizations had what they'd called "mottoes", which were short, easily remembered phrases that, in the minds of its recipients, spoke absolute truth about every single action and intention of the organization using it.

"The commies don't aspire to anything as lofty as either of those things," Gidal said. "We seek only to do one thing, and to do it well: keep the radio waves pure and alive."

Chapter 36. Return

The next morning, we all woke up at roughly the same time and went down for breakfast together. All the owner had was some granola and yogurt, which we were able to supplement with instant coffee from our MRE's and some random food like fruitcake and a cheese-like spread that came in a few MRE packs.

Over breakfast, we spoke in low tones about a few commie-related topics, mostly our individual set-ups. It was information we more or less already knew from idle chat on the konsole but it was nice to hear it again in person. Monster-b had been in the business for the longest, so his comm station sounded a lot like Rkicr's in the sense that it was well-organized, well-established, and filled with some of the best gear around. Maddawg's station was rather famous, among commies, being a patchwork of old and new gear, as he enjoyed using completely inappropriate old world technologies for new world purposes. Anomaly, or "Ana Molly", had merely been a hack of a handyman who would construct over-powered antennae so she could listen in on broadcasts that few others could reach, and ended up also constructing her own broadcast tower, which she would pack up and take closer to big radio stations so she could talk to the real commies inside. Now it looked like she had gotten a job from it.

It was easy to be impressed by these people, who got passionate about nothing more than radio waves and the ability to reach out and speak to people miles and miles across the land. And from that passion came service to others as well, since the world needed communication, it needed local news and warnings. It wanted communication. But not so much that it became mind-numbing; just the information that affected them or could affect them. That was what the commies were fighting for: doing one thing, and doing it well.

That idea had been pervasive across the land. The ability to do one thing well was all anyone ever really needed in life. Some people could plant seeds, others were more interested in harvesting. Some people could plan out roads while others preferred laying them. Some people could cook food, others could play music, or tell stories, or manage an inn, or repair broken things. And with everyone doing one of these things, the work became less demanding. There were plenty of people to provide for everyone's needs, as long as everyone provided for someone else. This was community.

And the community had built farms and cities and comm stations and radio towers and housing and inns and trading posts and cathedrals and bazaars. That was the new world, and no one owned it. Or, put another way, we all owned it.

After breakfast, we said our farewells and left the inn. Joe, the handyman, and I all traveled together for a short way until Joe had to turn on the main road to go back through the mountains. He'd go collect his things from his temporary home in the auto village, and continue upward back to his station.

The handyman and I continued back toward my mountaintop, a long but pleasant journey when you had someone to keep you company.

Chapter 37. Home

> To weld the people into one single
> unconquerable and all-destructive force – this
> is our aim, our conspiracy, and our task.
> — The Revolutionary's Catechism

When we arrived at my mountaintop, we found everything as I'd left it. It was well stocked and comfortable, and isolated. The handyman said she'd like that.

As for me, I was ready to be among people again, at least for a while. I wanted to meet people, and talk to them, and share ideas with them. I wanted to show them the new world's strengths and vibrancy. The new ideas, the new ways of doing things that should not be taken for granted.

This was my calling now, and so I stayed with the handyman a few complete moon cycles, until she felt confident in all of the duties of a commie. Most of it she already knew, at least in theory, and the largest learning curve was the use of the konsole, which tied all the hardware together and allowed the commie to control all communication in and out of their station. It had its own unique language which even in itself changed from konsole to konsole depending on what components had been used to build it.

But the handyman was a fast learner, and what I didn't have time to show her, she would learn from other commies as she went along. Operating a repeater tower was not considered a terribly glamourous job as commie jobs go; it was basically just taking someone else's information and archiving it and sending it back out. It wasn't creating broadcasts or archiving and analyzing drums and drums of Godstream, and it certainly wasn't inventing new ways of communicating or encrypting signals or anything fancy like that. If her tower was offline for a day or she missed a broadcast, the other repeaters and stations would hardly notice aside from maybe some degradation in signal quality or a delay in getting the broadcast out to their listeners.

So, when the handyman felt confident enough, I announced on the commie channels that Ender was being replaced for the time being with "anomaly" until otherwise noted. And then I packed up my bag again, and prepared to go out into the world and form a new kind of network.

Before I went, the handyman took her portable radio receiver out of her bag and gave it to me. "I figure you'll need this alot more than I do, now I got me a whole tower all t'myself."

"Thanks," I said, taking the radio.

"The Godstream's here," she said, pointing to a region on the dial. "But I guess you know that."

"I can generally find it," I said, the understatement glaringly obvious.

"Well, thanks," the handyman said. "And stay in touch if y'can."

"I'll listen to your broadcasts," I assured her. "And when I can, I'll ping you on the air."

And that was what I was, to the handyman, after I left. Something floating around in the air, out there, not in the great Devnull, not on the Godstream, but somewhere in between. Floating from station to station, infusing the commie ideals, the new world truths, and the new ways of communication. I was doing one thing, and I was doing it well.

And I will tell you one thing; I never returned to that mountain. It was Ana Molly's mountain before too long, she belonged on it like I had before her. Some day someone new would go there and she'd move on to a bigger comm station, maybe the one in KCG, maybe some other station.

But me, I was free, and floating, and the new world was spreading like a breath of fresh air. Even most cranks started calming themselves down into settlements, and Rkicr and his movement faded away from disinterest. Never again, we all decided together, would the ways of the old world pervade.

`Return Zero.`

Chapter 38. Credits

Story by Seth Kenlon

seth@straightedgelinux.com

Book, text, cover art, and audiobook are licensed cc-by-sa

creativecommons.org   [http://creativecommons.org/licenses/by-sa/3.0]

The Revolutionary's Catechism quotes were adapted from the Gutenberg Project's [http://gutenberg.org] etext of the pamphlet by Sergey Nechayev

The Audiobook version of this work features a Public Domain performance by the US Marine Band of Auld Lang Syne; for full audio book credits please listen to the audio book

Special Thanks to:

- Everyone in irc.freenode.net #oggcastplanet

- K5tux and Gort and a few others for radio consultation, which I pretty much ignored

- Bill von Hagen for xsltproc tips and a great .emacs file

- Linux Kernel developers, GNU, the Free Software Foundation, KDE at large, Norm Walsh and Docbook, perl, BASH, the Creative Commons, and everyone involved in and support of Free Software and free culture

- You, the reader

The audio book version of this work was read by Skirlet and produced by Klaatu. For full audio book credits, listen to the audio book.

Gear List

I always like hearing about the tools that artists used to get something done. So, for you technophiles and geeks out there: this book was written on Slackware Linux, mostly in Vim running in Konsole. Rsync -azv was my backup solution, no version control (I'm not advocating not using versioning, just being honest). The Slackermedia docbook workflow "Circulate" [http://slackermedia.info/circulate] was utilized. Two patches for bugs found during the production of this book were submitted to the open source txt2docbook project.

GODSTREAM.TAR

Listen to Godstream! A daring new
experimental album inspired by the
worlds of REVOLUTION RADIO and
PRIVATE PROPERTY.

Download your free copy of this and
more at http://aesdiopod.com/books
or
http://straightedgelinux.com/seth

As always, 100% Free Software
100% Creative Commons
100% Sci Fi

www.ingramcontent.com/pod-product-compliance
Lightning Source LLC
Chambersburg PA
CBHW030507260626
47157CB00005B/1689